LIFE AND LOVES IN SHINKLEY

Cover design by Jane Hodge

LIFE AND LOVES IN SHINKLEY

James Morley

Life and Loves in Shinkley
First published 2014

Published by Benhams Sea Mysteries, 1 Fir Cottage, Greatham, Liss,
Hampshire GU33 6BB
Typeset by John Owen Smith

ISBN 978-0-9548880-8-4

Printed by CreateSpace

CHAPTER 1

AUGUST 1973

Three weeks ago he had parted with the army and had become a civilian. Supposedly a free spirit, but in reality a nervous rootless individual searching for a job in a competitive world he hardly understood. If ever he needed the words of his old regimental motto it was now.

Simon Robsby parked the car in one of the visitors slots in front of the brick- built office. He looked around and he approved. The untidyness and lack of order in civilian business had often dismayed him; not so here. New tractors were lined as for a parade. Other agricultural machines were parked under lean-to buildings, and through the open doors of a workshop he could see the white sparks of an arc welder. Its operator was dressed in smart green overalls, as was the only other person in sight; a tall black man cleaning a BMW with a pressure washer.

Simon had been an infantry officer but had left the army after a course as a qualified engineer. He knew life from now on would be hard, especially getting a well-paid job; everyone said so. Why farm machinery? His father-in-law was a farmer, two hundred miles away in North Yorkshire where Simon had himself been born, forty-two years before. For seventeen of those years he had been married to Angie and for her, the service wife, it had been a hard slog of frequent uprooting house moves to soulless quarters and new schools; it had all been a long way from the permanence of her old home. She'd missed the farm, the animals and that certain rhythm of the seasons year after year. Angie never complained, but Simon knew she would not be entirely happy until they'd found security and home. He owed her a lot and the time had come to repay the debt. Once more he looked around. He felt increasingly warm towards this place and the job offer was the most promising yet: Sales Manager, with a starting salary of twenty thousand pounds before bonus. He needed the job and somehow he knew he would be happy here, but first he had to convince the boss man: the mysterious Mr Gladstone. Why did everyone collapse with mirth when asked if this Gladstone was related to the great Prime

Minister? To hell with them. Yorkshire man born and bred, he Simon, would be more than a match for these Southerners. As he walked purposefully toward the office door, he once again recited the regimental motto. He checked his smart suit and polished shoes straightened his tie and ran his fingers through his officer's cut blond hair. His watch read ten-thirty, minus eight seconds; nobody was going to fault him for punctuality.

This office seemed an austere place. The walls were plain white and decorated with the firm's tractor posters. The floor was polished wood and the only furniture a magazine-strewn table and four soft chairs. It was reminiscent of a dentist's waiting room.

'Wayne, darling, you're back!' a voice screamed almost in his ear.

Simon spun round; he'd missed the reception desk and the telephone switchboard to the right of the door. Behind the desk a teenage girl had half risen and was staring at him with a dazzling smile. Then the smile vanished and her face puckered with misery followed by a high-pitched wail.

'Ooh...I thought...I thought you were Wayne.' She was weeping now as she angrily pointed a finger at him.

The door of the inner office opened and to Simon's intense relief into the room came the one man he knew here: Peter Seldon the cherubic-faced workshop manager.

'Hello,' said Peter. 'I thought you soldier boys were supposed to fascinate the fair sex not send 'em into hysterics?'

'I thought he was Wayne,' sobbed the girl.

'Oh, God almighty, Sharon,' Peter Seldon sighed. He looked at Simon. 'That Wayne's a smarmy Uni-Parts salesman. He's been two timing our Sharon and a dozen more.'

'No...no!' the girl screamed.

'Yes, I tell you straight, Sharon. He's a waster, a slimeball, N.B.G.'

Simon looked at the pair gloomily. He'd psyched himself for this interview and now his resolution was fast being destroyed.

'Come on, Simon, governor's waiting for you.'

Simon pulled himself together, took a deep breath, and followed Peter Selden into the inner office. This room was almost as sparse as the reception, with more of the same posters and a prize plaque from the manufacturer whose franchise the firm held. In front of him was a large desk and laid out in order was his own certificate and CV. The only other person in the room was the man he had seen in the yard: the elegant black man cleaning the expensive motor. This individual was

at present pulling off his overalls and hanging them in a full-length locker. Simon puzzled over what sort of business allowed lower employees to store their dirty clothing in the managing director's sanctum. Or for that matter what sort of organisation would front itself with hysterical amateur dramatists like the one in reception. None of this squared with the well-ordered premises and the plaque on the wall.

'Peter, what's that God awful racket outside?' The black man addressed Selden.

Simon was surprised at the fellow's accent; it was that twangy, public school, senior officer speak, that always made his Northern hackles rise.

'That was Sharon,' said Peter. 'She thought our friend here was Wayne Stokes.'

'The Uni-Parts man? I've heard he's a bit of a snake-in-the-grass with the ladies.' Again that accent, a million miles from Barbados.

The black man turned and looked Simon up and down. 'My apologies, I don't know what you think of us, but I'm Bill Gladstone. I gather you're an army man.'

Simon, taking the proffered hand was aware that his eyes were staring and his jaw sagging.

Mr Gladstone was also staring. 'Have you a problem, Mr Robsby?' The voice had that patronising cadence that would have cut glass, but Simon was a good judge of character and here was a most formidable guy. He also had the sinking feeling that this interview was not going well. Once again he tried to draw on the regimental motto.

'No problems, I like this place,' he replied.

'I'm happy to hear it, but the question is, will we like you?'

Mr Gladstone reached under his desk and pulled out a discoloured length of metal. 'What that?'

'Track rod,'

'Is it safe?'

'No.'

'Why not?'

'Ball joint's knackered.'

Gladstone nodded. 'Where were your born?'

'In Whitby – Yorkshire.' Simon wished he knew where this was leading.

For the first time Gladstone smiled. 'Favourite haunt of Dracula, and Captain Cooke.'

'Yes.'

'I've mixed feelings about your Captain Cooke. You see my family comes from Sierre-Leone, not Cooke's stamping ground.'

'No,' Simon couldn't think of anything else to say.

'Yes, my ancestors were freed slaves. I have an inbred resentment of the likes of your Cooke, and you'll find I can be as bloody-minded as any Yorkshire man.'

'You can say that again,' Peter winked defusing the tension. 'Don't let Bill wind you up. He was born in bloody Winchester, posh school, Cambridge, the lot.'

'Yes, we've come a long way,' mused Gladstone. 'What's the predominant soil type to the north of this town?' The mood had changed again as he flashed the question. 'Come on now; what plough would you use with our two hundred horsepower model?'

'Three furrow reverse,' Simon guessed in desperation.

'Big deal,' Gladstone grinned. 'My kid's pedal tractor would pull that out there.' He and Peter exchanged glances. 'Never mind let's try something else…'

Simon had that nasty feeling of being cornered and already this much-prized job seemed to be slipping from his grasp. Gladstone was eyeing him sardonically, evidently weighing up the next question. In the outer office the telephone was ringing; in fact it had been ringing for almost half a minute.

Mr Gladstone, apparently losing interest in Simon, listened with a frown.

'Why doesn't that girl answer? Nothing makes a worse impression than an unmanned switchboard.'

At last Simon saw his opportunity, and he grasped it. He stood and strode through the door. Sharon was slumped, head on table, moaning feebly. He reached over and picked up the telephone.

'Gladstone Engineering. How can I help you? Yes, certainly. He may be in a meeting but I'll see if I can get him for you.' Simon flicked the silence switch and walked back into the office.

Both Gladstone and Selden were grinning.

'You know,' said Gladstone, 'that was good, very good, I like your style. Is that army training?'

Simon relaxed and smiled. 'Our regimental motto is, *Be Resolute*, and I've often found it helps.'

'Well, your resolution has done you a power of good this time. Forget the interview, if you want the job it's yours.'

CHAPTER 2

'Angie, I've done it. Got the job.' Simon had gone straight to a phone box and rung home in Yorkshire.

'Well done. What are the people like?'

'Well, they're Southerners of course but still nice.'

She laughed. 'It's all right for you. I've gotta' mix with their wives; all Southern lah di dah.'

'Well, the boss man's missus, probably, but the others seem normal working class lads.'

Angie laughed again. 'Then how long before they find out you were an officer?'

'I think the boss man knows that already. Anyway I'm going house hunting.'

Simon climbed back in his car and drove into the nearby county town. This Southern cathedral city was impressive, with its streets that seemed to radiate out from a central hub cantering on the tall spire medieval cathedral. The place had warmth so different to the harsh Northern cities. Simon's spirits lifted. Yes, he could be happy here. He began to trawl the estate agents. He was looking for a three bedroom country cottage in a rural setting and not too far from his work place. He came away with a number of brochures but he needed to actually visit each house with Angie. Would these Southerners really be so different in culture? So far the people he had met seemed normal by any standards. In fact the men appeared cheerful, or more so than most Yorkshire men, and the girls were prettier. Of course this was all a bit of a sweeping observation. He could make a real conclusion when he'd been around these parts for a few months.

He parked his car in the yard behind the hotel and walked into the saloon bar. 'Pint o' Mason's bitter, love,' he told the bar girl.

'I say, I say,' said a voice, definitely cut glass and Southern. 'I see and hear a Northerner.'

Simon was mildly annoyed as he swung round to face the voice. It was the sound of all those officers from superior regiments. Well he was now Simon Robsby, Major retired and wasn't about to be intimidated.

He assumed his most irritating voice, or irritating to these

Southerners. 'Aye, lad, I'm Yorkshire. You sounds a bit Surrey...'

The other did not look the Guards officer type. He was tall certainly, but wore a dark suit that had seen better days. The man was handsome in a way with dark features and jet black hair. His face was framed by a dark beard. Whatever this character was he was unlikely to be a soldier. 'No, not Surrey. I'm a Sussex man although my parents were foreign. Sorry I'd better introduce myself. I'm Daniel Lederman.' Mr Lederman held out his hand. Simon was mollified and shook it. The man had a really friendly grin and that alone was defusing Simon's prejudice.

'I'm Simon Robsby. Yes I'm from Yorkshire but I'm going to be working here now,'

'Oh, you'll find us a sociable lot even if we do vote Tory. May I ask what your job here is?'

'It's no secret. I'm going to sell tractors.'

'Would that be for Bill Gladstone?'

'Yes, that's right. I like him.'

'Everyone likes Bill, except the BPP of course and they don't like anyone much – certainly don't like the likes of me.'

The British Purity Party; Simon had heard of this racist neo-fascist rabble. They had not gained much support in the industrial north. He knew their alleged leader came from somewhere around these parts in the south.

'Well,' he said. 'Bill might be black but I've never met anyone more British.' He paused. 'You said the BPP wouldn't like you?'

'Oh yes, you see I'm worse than black, much worse. My father was a refugee from Poland and we're dastardly Jews.'

'I thought all that had gone with the Nazis.'

Lederman shook his head and looked grim. 'The BPP are Nazis.'

Simon was still puzzled. 'My CO was Colonel Cohen. One of the best. We reckoned he's on his way to being CGS. That's head of the whole army.'

'Not if Wally Fircomb can stop it. Wally is the chief of the BPP and he lives at Shinkley not far from here.' He grinned. 'You're an army guy?'

'That's right. I've only just retired. Second Northumbrian Fusiliers, major.'

Lederman laughed. 'A major. I tell you, go in any village pub around here and ask "is the major in tonight?" There'll always be one.'

Simon found himself liking this odd character more and more.

'Well there'll be another one now.'

Daniel Lederman drank his beer. 'You're Simon; that sounds a bit Yiddish?'

'Sorry, can't help you there. We're all Methodists where I come from.'

Daniel yawned and wished Simon a restful night. Simon, in spite of his first impression liked this character but was still a bit mystified. But as a Yorkshire man he was not restrained from asking questions. He turned to the bar tender. 'That guy seemed nice. Can you tell me anything about him?'

'What, old Dan. He's a joker, bit of a comedian. He lives in Hope Street. His old dad's the rabbi in the temple or whatever. Dan's missus edits the local rag. Their little girl's an actress. She's played a part in the big theatre across the way.'

Simon went to bed that night but spent an hour mugging up on the Gladstone range of tractors and farm machinery. This was expensive advanced stuff compared with the machines one saw in Yorkshire. No doubt he would be dealing with snobbish titled land owners, bankers, and ex-guards officers. For now he would rather relax and have a night's good sleep.

CHAPTER 3

That morning he found their new house. Of course he would need Angie to approve but he knew she would love it. He was in the village of Shinkley Common and in the main street was this three bed cottage with off-street parking and a nice big garden. He found a phone box and called Angie. 'Sweetheart, I've found our house.' He told her the details but could not hide his enthusiasm.

'I'm longing to see it already,' she laughed. 'Anyway you've suffered years of married quarters, so I guess you know what we would all like.'

'I'd better go,' he replied. 'I can see the estate agent bloke waving. Slimy smooth Southerner...'

Angie laughed. 'Go and do a Yorkshire deal.'

The slimy agent in fact looked more bored than anything and they agreed a deal that would swallow a fair bit of Simon's army redundancy but leave the family with a modest mortgage. Next he found his way to the village pub. It was called THE WINDY SHIP and was a traditional build Sussex house. The bar was not long open for the midday session. A pretty barmaid served him his pint and he settled in a corner with a small table.

'Who be you then?' a voice came from out of the gloom. Simon peered forward and now he saw he was not alone at the table. In a dark corner by the curtained window was a wizened figure of an old man.

'Sorry, there,' said Simon. 'I never saw you.'

'You talks funny. You a Scotch jock?'

Simon couldn't help it and laughed. 'I don't come from these parts but I'm from up north – Yorkshire.'

'Yorkie, are you? We beat you at cricket.'

'Not that often, I think. Tell me, are you local.'

'Me, lived in Shinkley all my life.'

Well, this man could be useful. 'My names's Robsby, Simon Robsby. I going to be living here soon I hope and working locally.'

'Well, this ain't a bad old place to live. What be your line as they say on the telly.'

'I'm selling tractors and farm gear.'

'Would that be for Black Bill?'

'Yes, Bill Gladstone he signed me up yesterday.'

The old man drained his beer and Simon tactfully paid for the refill. 'Yeah, everyone likes Bill. He may be black but he's a gent, not like some around here.'

Simon grinned. 'Tell me more.'

The old man gave a wheezing laugh. 'Where do I start?'

'Well, who lives in that big pile on the hill? You know the one with the long drive and those iron gates.'

'That be old Rufus Blanner.'

'Not the MP?'

'That be him. Pompous old bastard.'

'I don't go much on politicians myself. I've been a soldier and they're the ones that send us to be shot at.'

'Blanner's his name, but we all call him Blabbermouth.'

'Why vote for him then?'

'Good question. I don't I'm a Labour man but round here them's all Tories, even the working class lads touch their caps all polite like.'

'That's what they call a safe seat then?'

'Maybe, but Mr Kellingham at the other end o' the village, he runs the Liberals in these parts and he reckons as they could give Blabbermouth a bit o' a run.'

Simon wanted to move the conversation away from politics. 'Can you tell me anything about the farmers? They're the ones I'll be dealing with.'

'Well, there's the big boys. You know the thousand acre lot and then there's smaller ones with cows and pigs. Reckon old Bill'll want you to go for the biguns.'

Simon finished his drink and stood. 'You've been very helpful, Mr err?'

The wizened old man shifted a little way from the window. 'I'm Barney. Everyone around of here knows Barney. As you work for Bill I'm pleased to be of help like.'

Simon left the pub and took his car on a further drive around the neighbourhood. He still had forty-eight hours and a weekend ahead. On Monday he would report to the Gladstone premises for his first day's employment. He was growing to like this Sussex countryside. It had a warmth very different from the Dales near where he had been raised. This was a landscape of woods and trees, broad fields and little villages that seemed hardly changed from medieval times. Everywhere to the north the landscape was dominated by the oddly named

13

Downs; the long range of hills that dated to the very formation of the earth. He was still a Northerner and proud to be so, but he felt he could be at home here and that this was the right place to rear his children. On Monday he was due at Gladstone's Agricultural for an intensive briefing on their tractors and machinery. This would be a challenge but interesting. The tractors on his wife's family's farm were all ten-years-old. The massive machines in the Gladstone's yard were in a different league.

He paused in the street opposite the village school. This is where Lizzie and Mark would be spending their early learning days, well Mark anyway; Lizzie would be in secondary school. How would they fit in with these Southern kids? Different upbringing, speaking with different accents; would they be bullied? Well probably some of the local young ones might try it on but his two were army kids and well able to look after themselves. And anyway, hadn't they already faced enough house moves and new schools. Well, now that would be over. What on earth was that place over there? He could see what would be an upmarket house up a short driveway. It was sturdy 1930s architecture but why have that enormous banner across the front door?

He strained his eyes and read: *SISTERHOOD OF ENGLAND WE WILL NOT BE MOVED.* What the hell did that mean? Simon wondered if he should go back to the pub and find the grumpy Barney. Well it was none of his business and he had plenty of time to settle into the scene at Shinkley Common.

CHAPTER 4

That Monday Simon was wholly absorbed in tractor manuals, tractor maintenance, combine harvester capacities and a dozen other items from chain saws to water pumps.

His army training really did help now. He was used to absorbing facts and supporting information. This was new territory, yes, but he absorbed it all like a sponge. He still took a heavy file of paperwork back with him to the hotel. Well, tomorrow Angie would be joining him with the kids and in ten days time they could take possession of their Shinkley Common house.

He really liked Bill Gladstone. His new employer was not the run of the mill public school type. He could get his hands dirty on an oily engine along with his workers. Bill was encouraging and had complimented Simon on his ability to absorb all this technical know how. Returning to the hotel that evening he saw Daniel Lederman. He had been told that Mrs Lederman edited the local paper so Daniel was a useful man to know. Simon bought the man a beer and then asked.

'What can you tell me about Shinkley Common?'

'Shinkley,' Daniel laughed. 'It's the centre of politics in this region.'

'Yes, I understand the MP Blanner lives there. They showed me his house.'

'Yes,' Daniel replied. 'Blabbermouth, funny old fellow and well named; opens his mouth before he thinks too often. As far as we can gather Blabbermouth would do away with the old age pension and the health service and bring back the workhouse. I think his Westminster whips can't wait for him to retire. Blabbermouth doesn't like the Common Market so he's defying Edward Heath. But then there's Hugh Kellingham. He's the chairman of the constituency Liberals and he lives in the Shinkley High Street. I suppose we've got to include that shit Fircomb...'

'What, you mean the BPP guy?'

'That's him, noisy little Fascist. Lives on the outskirts of the village. Luckily he doesn't have much support there.'

'I don't want to get mixed up with any politics. Bill Gladstone wouldn't like that. But tell me, the place opposite the school with the

banner on the front...'

'My wife would be more help to you there. You mean the sisterhood, and I can tell you they would shrivel you up on two counts. You're a man which is bad enough but you've been a soldier and that's almost worse.'

'They're sisters?'

'No none of them are related as far as I know; they're a commune. There's three of them; all virgin spinsters and proud of it. Plus one poor little girl that they're fostering.'

Simon was even more puzzled. 'Virgin spinsters? That must seem odd these days.'

'Oh, you haven't heard the whole of it. Think: all men are evil, all men are rapists, every sex act is a rape.'

Simon laughed. 'You know they live within a stone's throw of Rufus Blanner the MP.'

'Oh yes, that lecherous old goat. He's the misogynist of all misogynists. He's old now but he's on his fifth marriage. Mrs Blanner, the current one, is thirty years younger than the old bloke. I imagine the sisterhood sitting around their witches fire are cursing him every night.'

Simon laughed. 'I'd better not tell my missus about Mr Blanner's girl, not that she's a jealous type.' Simon had his own dark secret. He saw a mental picture of Melina and Angie must never know.

Lederman grinned. 'Watch out for all those farmer's daughters.'

'I've been warned. Right, what can you tell me about Solvington farms?'

Lederman laughed. 'My God, after we've just mentioned gorgeous farmer's daughters.'

'Why, will there be a group of them?'

'Quite the opposite. Solvington House is the home of Lady Reece-Lamprey...'

'I've heard that name.'

'I bet you have. Lady R- L campaigns the length and breath of the UK to raise morals. To put it bluntly she wants to ban sex and rock music which are just about the only things most people are interested in.'

Simon remembered. 'That's the old girl who had some sort of rally in Scarborough a few months back. Never heard how many went.'

'More than you may suppose I would guess. The puritans are back and we'd all better watch out.'

'Thanks for the warning. Bill Gladstone's set me to call on

Solvington farms. I've been ask to check they're happy with their big combine. But he's told me to find a manager, bloke called Mortlish.'

'That's a funny name. Wonder how he fares with Lady L.'

Simon found Solvington Farms Estate following two wrong turns and a stop to ask directions. He steered his car carefully up a potholed lane that ended in a well-appointed farmyard with barns and fields full of dairy cows. He found the estate office and was shown in to the manager, Mr Mortlish. Mortlish was a small, bald headed man dressed in jeans and a check shirt. 'Hello there, you must be old Bill's new salesman. Mortlish spoke with the same rolling southern accent that Simon heard everywhere.

'That's right, I'm Simon Robsby. Mr Gladstone says you need some combine spares.'

'Yes, hang on and I'll give you the details.' Mortlish rummaged in some files and pulled out a typed sheet of paper. 'Here you are. These two drive belts needed before harvest and the cab ventilation needs some work.'

'That's all right. We'll have an engineer out to you this week.'

Mortlish grinned. 'Got time for a cup of coffee?'

'Thanks. I'd like that.'

Mortlish walked to a corner of the office and sorted two cups and filled an electric kettle. 'You're not from these parts I guess,' he said.

Simon no longer felt defensive. 'No, I'm from Yorkshire.'

'I'm Carl, by the way. I'm a bit of a foreigner myself even though I'm Sussex born. My real surname is Miltenheim. My dad was a German POW working on farms and never went home. He married my mum, she's the Mortlish, who was a local girl and I'm one of five kids born here in Sussex.' He handed Simon a cup of coffee and offered a bowl of sugar lumps.

Simon took a sip of the hot tea, 'Well, you've done well for yourself. But after all we're all descended from migrants going back a few thousand years. My ancestors were Vikings and I would guess a pretty nasty lot. And then of course there's our great Mr Bill Gladstone.'

Carl Mortlish nodded. 'Can't fault Bill, he's one of the best. Even my boss lady likes him.'

'Would that be Lady Reece-Lamprey?'

'Oh, you've heard of her then and the LOD.'

'The what?'

Carl laughed, 'The League of Decency. You know, dire punish-

ment for teenage sex and hangings for homos.'

'Is she connected with the females here in Shinkley Common? That's where we're going to live by the way.'

'You mean the witches coven. I don't think they get on that well with her ladyship. Rumour is they're a bunch of lesbies.'

Simon liked this man. His prejudices against southerners were almost gone now. Really they weren't so very different to the people back home. Now what did he mean by that? This was now their home and he'd better get used to it. There followed a happy half hour while Carl took him on a tour of the farm buildings and Simon took notes of the tractors and other machinery. He could see why this estate was one of Bill's best customers. Carl liked to trade-in any tractor with more than a certain number of hours on the clock. Simon understood that the accounts were handled in another office in Lady Reece-Lamprey's stately home. He was feeling a little ambivalent about meeting her in the future. Although he felt he had a blameless family life he had been led and fallen into temptation before in army overseas locations. He could never forget Cyprus and the lovely sexy Melina. Melina, yes and Angie must never know.

He drove back to the hotel and there in the car park was the familiar and battered Ford Anglia. He ran into the hotel foyer and there was his Angie and their two kids: fourteen-year-old Lizzie and twelve-year-old Mark. He hugged all of them feeling a sudden rush of happiness. Tomorrow he would take the whole family to see their new home.

CHAPTER 5.

'Oh, it's lovely – so cute.' Angie stood in the driveway of her new home her eyes sparkling. The two children were racing around the garden with yelps of excitement.

Simon put an arm around her. 'Bit of a step up from married quarters.'

'When can we move in?'

'Agent says as soon as we've completed the legal stuff – be about eight days' time.'

Angie looked concerned. 'How is this new job going?

'I like it. It's all tractors and farm gear and the people are great.'

'So, you believe you'll stick it long-term?'

'Yes, I can't see anything better coming along. I'm here for as long as it takes.'

Angie nodded. 'What are the people like around here – Southerners..?'

'Oh they're all right. I think we Yorkies are a bit isolated. The people here; honestly, they don't seem a lot different. At least not once you've got used to the accent. Come on, I've got the keys – let's have a look indoors.'

'Hello there,' a cheery voice sounded from the entry gate. Simon turned and saw a tall man badly in need of a haircut. He was dressed in a smart business suit but without a tie.

'I say,' he called. 'Are you our new neighbours?'

'Talk about accents,' Angie whispered. 'Right plummie Southerner.'

'Hello,' Simon called. 'Yes we move in a week or two.' He strode down the short drive to the gate. He held out his hand and the stranger shook it. 'We're the Robsbys, I'm Simon and this is Angela.'

'I'm Hugh Kellingham,' replied the other. 'You must be the chap who's working for our Bill Gladstone.'

'That's right.'

'Bill is a great man. We're hoping he'll stand for us at the next election.'

'Stand?'

'Oh I'd better explain. I'm chair of our constituency Liberals. We

19

think a candidate of the calibre of Bill could shake things up a bit. Excuse me but do you have any political allegiance?'

'No, I've only just left the army and we don't entirely trust politicians even if we have to go and fight for them.'

The man chuckled. 'Well, they can't send you to war now and if you want a better type of politician, well we can chose some.'

'I'm not sure my boss would want to be an MP.'

'Well, chances are he wouldn't get there. Tory party rules the roost in these parts, but a candidate like Bill would shake things up even if we didn't make it all the way.'

'Is Mr Gladstone involved in your party?'

'Oh yes, he's our constituency president and with a name like Gladstone there's only one party colour he could be.'

Simon was not sure he wanted to know too much about all this. Kellingham seemed a decent guy; but party politics in this strange new country was not for him. He had never really taken an interest in it anyway. In Yorkshire it always seemed to be a contest between grand land-owning families, Tory, and disgruntled trade unionists Labour. Simon had no feelings for either.

'Your children seem happy,' said Kellingham. 'Have you checked out schools? If you want I can help you there.'

'Thanks you, yes. The girl Elizabeth is fourteen and she's been at a comprehensive, Mark is only just twelve; so how do you rate the village school over there?'

'Oh, we like it. Mrs Hanbury is the head and she is good. You know progressive but well in control. My kids all went there, in fact the youngest Tamsine is still there. She's very gifted with music and we're hoping she'll be accepted at Bedales.'

'Where?' Simon was a bit out of his depth.

'Independent school near Petersfield. That's in Hampshire a few miles north of here.'

So, Simon mused. This Mr Kellingham wasn't short of a bob or two. His own kids had had a mixed education in various military and state schools. Now, perhaps they too could settle down in a more permanent and stable life.

'Excuse me, Mr Kellingham...'

'Oh no, Please call me Hugh.'

'Thank you, Hugh. But I was going to say that this seems a very politically minded village. There's Mr Blanner, and you, and the ladies in that house over there...'

'Oh, you mean the Sisterhood. They invited Chris, my wife, to

meet them but told her that to join them she would have to ditch me and the children, hate men and swear sexual abstinence for life. Well, I think women should have complete equality but there are limits and rational ways of achieving the goal.'

'I was told by someone that the BPP are active as well...'

Hugh looked grim. 'Fircomb, their national leader lives just outside our village down Long-Copse Lane. I dread to think what ranting he'll do if Bill stands for us here.'

Simon nodded 'Black man of course.'

'Nobody could be much more English than Bill. Fircomb is a brain-dead fanatic. I'm told he's got a portrait of Hitler in his front room.'

Christ, thought Simon. The BPP must be a Nazi revival. He felt genuinely shocked and worried. 'Does anyone around here take him seriously?'

'Not around here, no, but he's building a following in the big cities.'

Simon introduced Hugh to Angie and the children and was in turn invited to have dinner with the whole Kellingham family as soon as they were settled in their new home. Then they drove back into town to their hotel.

CHAPTER 6

Simon was finding his way at Gladstones and was far more relaxed. Peter Seldon had given him an advance briefing on the new super-tractor that was about to be added to the range. All this would be fine had not Simon been disturbed by the attitude of Sharon the reception-ist. Her fury with him on their first acquaintance had developed into something else. The silly girl kept looking at him with a soulful doe-eyed expression and insisted on making him cups of tea. He supposed that he should be flattered by this attention but he didn't want Angie to suspect anything, particularly as he had no interest in this girl and certainly not after the hysterics of the other day. Now he was due at that solicitor's office to complete the formalities for their new house. With his army pension, let alone his salary with Gladstone, he could afford the deposit and mortgage without Angie having to go out to work. That would be her choice of course; he had more sense than to dictate to his wife. He had learned something over the years.

He parked his car in the little backyard behind the solicitor's office and walked the few yards to the entrance. Inside he could hear a raised voice, shrill and high-pitched in anger. He pushed open the ornate carved front door and walked inside. Behind the front desk sat a young girl receptionist with a white faced shell-shocked expression. Leaning towards her was a figure as bizarre as anything Simon had ever seen. She was a woman, probably late thirties, dressed in a full-length flower pattern gown. Around her head was a strange floral head band and he noticed her feet were bare. Well, it was summer and warm – not nice but so what? The woman turned and glared at him with that cold hostility Simon had not experienced since he'd crossed the drill sergeant at Sandhurst.

'What the hell are you doing here, man?' she half spat at him in a strong East Coast American accent.

'Sorry,' Simon was conciliatory. 'I'm here to do some business, but don't let me intrude. You were here first.'

The woman turned abruptly and bent forward again. 'I want to see Amelia. This is women's business. We don't need men for this or for anything else if it comes to that.'

The receptionist looked near to tears. 'Oh, please Ms Shartcroft.

22

Mrs Allington is out and there's only Mr Rikkards in the office, but as I said he has all the papers.'

'No,' replied the woman. 'I won't see that sneering man. Let me know when Amelia is free. That is if that husband of hers ever lets her any freedom.' She swung around and renewed her hostile stare. 'So, who are you?'

'He's Major Robsby, a client of ours,' said the receptionist.

'Major, did you say Major – are you a trained killer?'

Simon couldn't help it. He laughed. 'Well, I'm not Salvation Army.'

'War is evil. All men are evil – throw away their guns now!' Ms Shartcroft left without a backward glance.

'Oh, I'm so sorry about all that,' the girl receptionist shook her head and grimaced.

'Who was that and what's biting her? She must be insane.'

'She Ms Shartcroft she's the head of the Shinkley Sisterhood…'

'Oh,' said Simon. 'I've seen their house and the banner over the front door. Why do they hate men? Have they all been disappointed at some time?'

'I really couldn't say, but I don't get it. I've got a steady boyfriend and he's sweet, but I daren't ever tell the Shartcroft that.' She smiled. 'I'll go and see if Mr Rikkards is ready to see you.' The girl rose to her feet and darted through a side door. He could not make head nor tail of this last confrontation. It looked as if Shinkley, with the BPP as well, was a bit of a madhouse.

In less than a minute the receptionist was back and ushered Simon into the inner office.

'The house is ours, love.' Simon kissed his wife. 'We can get the furniture movers on the go and be in there in three days time.'

The family furnishings were all in a store near Salisbury, the family having evacuated the Bulford married quarters. They had enough spare cash as well to buy some more choice items to complete their new home.

'How did the school search go?' Simon asked.

'The village school have a place for Mark as soon as term starts in September. We've put Lizzie down for the comprehensive in the town here.'

'I've heard good things about the village school but do we know much about the other one?'

'Well, it seems they're good at sport and they've had several kids

qualify for university; one even went to Cambridge.'

'Can't see Lizzie going there somehow.'

Angie laughed. 'How can you say that? She's a clever girl. Tell you something else. They've got an army cadet company.'

'That'll be good for them, but I'm not really sure about them joining the service.'

Angie frowned. 'Personally I'd rather they did jobs in civvy street, but it'll be their choice.'

Simon checked his watch. 'I'd better go. I'm due to sell a tractor, or try to.'

Angie smiled. 'Do you get a bonus if you sell one?'

'Maybe, but I earn the boss's goodwill and maybe a salary increase in the new-year.'

'Right, that's good. You go to it.'

Simon was due at Hammer Cross Farm a substantial arable unit to the north of the town.

He took a diversion through Shinkley to have another look at their new house. It was a delight to see, sitting there in the sunlight with its short driveway and garden trees and shrubs. It couldn't be more different from the drab functional service quarters.

Hammer Cross Farm also couldn't have been more different from the farms Simon knew in his home country. In the Dales, farmers now had milking machines and small tractors but apart from a few grand estates agriculture was all small units run by hard working families. Here in the south he was encountering huge complex sites with smart offices. He parked his car in a marked bay and collected his sales leaflets. The farm office was a modern brick built building. Within were desks with modern word processors and a teleprinter. All this was presided over by a well-spoken young man who to Simon seemed more a juvenile, even teenager. Simon explained who he was and the boy called someone on a portable radio. The boy grinned. 'Robbie in the workshops will talk to you now. I'll show you where.'

Simon followed the youth across a wide concrete expanse flanked by covered yards with cattle in. In front of them he could see a vast modern building reminiscent of an aircraft hanger. They entered through a wide double door and into an interior crowded with machines. On one side stood two enormous combine harvesters and around them were pick-up balers and an odd looking contraption that Simon knew was for making the new style big bales. Three small tractors were parked although there were empty spaces that Simon

guessed were for others outside working in the fields. After the bright sunlight outside this place seemed dark apart from the sparks from an arc welder in a far corner. This was wielded by a squat figure with head enveloped in a protective mask.

'Oi, Robbie,' yelled the youth. 'Gentleman to see you from Gladstones.'

The man put down his welder and removed the mask. 'You here to sell us summat?'

'Mr Robsby, this is Robbie, or rather he's Mr Ramshaw our chief engineer.'

Simon had reacted to the gruff voice of the welding man. His intonation was pure north country. 'Hello, Mr Ramshaw, I guess you come from my neck of the woods.'

Ramshaw was grinning now. 'You a Yorkie? takes one to know one as they say.'

'God's own country,' Simon grinned. 'Though it's not a bad country in these parts.'

'Aye, heard of you,' said the man. 'You working at Gladstones?'

'That's right; would you like a better tractor?'

'Wouldn't mind. What've you got?'

Simon spread out his brochures on a work bench and explained the attributes of the new four by four high horsepower tractor. He pointed out the advanced instrumentation and the completely new heating and air conditioning system in the cab. His fellow Yorkshireman maintained an impassive expression throughout, which was only to be expected.

'You'd best talk the money angle to the boss,' said Robbie. 'Eh, Nige, you think your dad'll dig in his pocket for this one?'

'I'll twist his arm,' said the boy.

Boss's son, thought Simon. The estate belonged to the Earl of Hocklington, so this callow boy must be a Lord as well. This South country still had surprises in store.

'Does his Lorship take the financial decisions then?' said Simon.

'Oh aye, but if I says it's a good buy he'll cough up the cash. Any road we could do with more power at ploughing time.'

'Let me have a drive,' said the boy, 'and I'll twist his arm all right.'

Simon with this son and heir returned to the office and they filled in the purchase forms leaving only a signature needed.

'How soon can you make a delivery?' asked the boy.

'We've four coming in the yard next week.'

CHAPTER 7

'They're coming, they're coming,' Lizzie was jumping up and down pointing at the big box van turning into the driveway.

'That's the furniture firm,' said Simon. 'The bulk of our stuff'll be along in an hour or two.'

This was their great day, the one where the whole family took possession of the first home they had ever owned. Just arriving was the local van with their new sofa and armchair set, plus a dining table.

'One good thing,' said Simon. 'Bill's given me a fifty percent discount on a new lawn mower. Seems he's pleased with me over that tractor sale.'

'Dad, can we play with it?' asked Mark.

'No you blooming well cannot. Wait a few years and you'll be right fed up having to do the garden.'

'There speaks the voice of military authority,' Angie laughed.

The family spent a strenuous but happy day breathing life into their new home. The two furniture vans arrived from Wiltshire and gradually the house filled with all the familiar things that had accompanied them through half a dozen previous moves. This time, thought Simon, they would have to carry him out in a coffin before he consented to move again. As the last van departed they saw a familiar figure by the entrance gate, their neighbour Hugh Kellingham.

'Hello there,' he called.

Simon raised a hand in acknowledgement and walked across to greet him. 'Simon,' said Hugh. 'My wife and I would like you to come to dinner with us this evening.'

Simon glanced at Angie who had now joined them. 'We'd love to,' said Angie. 'But we've the two children to put to bed.'

'Well, we eat at seven, so why not bring them; our three will be eating with us anyway.'

The Kellingham family lived at the far end of the Shinkley street. Simon and Angie plus the two kids drove the quarter mile and found the right house. It lay up a short entry drive and had an air of prosperity about it. Simon noted a tennis court and well maintained lawns, trees and shrubs. The house at the end of the drive was another

spacious 1930s design similar to their new one and the one lived in by the Shinkley Sisterhood.

Simon parked the car by the front door. Nearby standing watching them was a rather scruffy small boy. He was aged around ten and dressed in grubby T-shirt, shorts and flipflops. The boy ambled across to them as Simon wound down the driver side-window.

'All right then; who are you?' demanded the child.

Simon was a trifle thrown by this but Angie was a quick to react. 'This gentleman is the King of Sweden and I am Miss Raquel Welsh.'

'King, you say. Where's 'is crown?'

A woman had emerged through the front door. She was around forty, Simon guessed, and still good-looking with styled blonde hair. 'Max,' she spoke to the boy. 'That wasn't a nice greeting now was it.'

'Naah, 'spose not,' the child replied. 'Bloke says e's a king but e' can't be – not driving a flipping Anglia.'

'Now, Max, that's not nice. These are our evening guests.'

'Oh, all right, but he's not a king and she ain't a film star.'

'Max, would you please go indoors and tell father the guests are here.'

The boy Max ran indoors and the lady looked apologetic. 'Oh, I'm Christine Kellingham. I'm so sorry that Max was a bit rude but we encourage self-expression and relevant awareness. We never shout at the children and try to reason with them.'

And probably bring up a nest of clever criminals, thought Simon.

'Please come indoors all of you,' said Christine.

The house was lit and full of a mix of antique and modern furniture. This family was clearly wealthy, but where the money came from was not clear. Christine led them into a spacious lounge and there stood Hugh his face smiling in welcome. 'Have a drink,' he said waving a wine bottle. Now Simon was able to have a good look at their host. He was tall, slim and striking looking with wavy dark hair. Christine the wife was also tall with blonde hair tied back in a pony tail. They were clearly an eccentric pair, and family if it came to that, and they were as different as could be from Simon's Yorkshire background.

They both accepted drinks. The wine was a fine quality red and Simon accepted a second glass. On this occasion Angie would drive them all home.

Hugh addressed his wife. 'How is Cassandra getting on in the kitchen?'

'She told me ten minutes,'

'Cassie's our eldest,' said Hugh. 'She's cooking dinner for us all.'

'You can come and sit down anyway,' called a detached voice from the open door.

They followed Hugh and Christine into a dining room. There stood a polished wood table with odd looking chairs. Must be art deco or some sort, thought Simon. A girl had entered from what was clearly the kitchen. She was pretty, fair-haired and aged around seventeen, dressed in a flowing off-shoulder dress topped by a green overall bib. 'Soup first,' she said. 'Then it's beef, but I won't eat that...'

'Cassie's a vegetarian,' said Christine.

'All my group are,' said the girl. 'I suppose all you lot are carnos.'

'What?' Simon was puzzled.

'I mean you love killing poor little animals.'

'What about rats?' asked Hugh grinning.

Cassandra pulled a face. 'They're disgusting. I hate them.'

'I think they're sweet,' said a new voice. A younger girl child had entered the room. She was clearly the sister but was probably around eight-years-old. 'I'm Tammie,' she introduced herself. 'Max is coming down in a minute. I've told him to have a shower and dress in respectables.'

Simon still felt mildly baffled by this family. His own children were standing behind their mother looking puzzled and embarrassed. These new friends, both Southern and totally non-military must be a huge culture shock. The boy Max appeared now dressed in fashion jeans and a white shirt. He and his elder sister served the family and guests. The food was plain and excellent; nothing over fancy and continental. Simon felt almost back home. The conversation was genuinely interesting and Simon was much relieved that politics was never mentioned. He learned that Hugh was a high executive in the film industry and a trustee of the nearby Memorial Theatre. The Kellinghams were close friends with the Gladstones looking back over many years. Bill Gladstone owned a racing yacht on the nearby harbour and the Kellinghams crewed for him at Cowes and other racing events.

Despite the uncertain beginning the evening went well, and Simon and Angie began to really like these new friends. After the meal all the children ran into the garden and played noisily. Simon was uncertain whether he wanted his two to be over-close to this unruly brood, but Angie seemed happy enough and she was always a better judge than he to the children's welfare. Finally they left for home having invited their hosts to dinner once they had settled into their new house.

CHAPTER 8

Did he still miss service life? Simon had occasional pangs of regret but fewer and fewer as the weeks passed. The family were settling into the rhythm of life in Shinkley Common and were making more friends. Above all Simon loved his new job. He really had fallen on his feet this time. Gladstones were good employers and all the people working there were very much a team. Simon sold another high horsepower tractor to the obvious delight of Bill. In the hot weather of that summer Sharon the receptionist wore flaunting summer dresses and still sometimes made eyes at him. Peter Seldon made ribald comments. 'Don't take too much notice. Sharon's a good girl most of the time. We'll find her a nice young guy and that'll settle her down.' Simon sincerely hoped so.

Happily local politics did not intrude much. The family were on increasingly friendly terms with the Kellinghams and once when Simon was making a visit to the estate farm of Rufus Blanner he met the M.P. in person. Blanner was a mildly corpulent figure with red face and a shock of untidy grey hair. He had barely deigned to speak to Simon and had communicated through his manager who stood beside him looking both respectful and embarrassed. Then on another afternoon Simon had driven back to the office to find the entrance blocked by a mob of banner waving thugs. A stereotype skinhead had stood in front of the car and thumped on the bonnet. 'You,' the thug shouted. 'You're a white man. Why d'you work for a blackie?' Simon looked around and saw the banners were all for the BPP. He wasn't sure what their leader Fircomb looked like and he didn't want to know. He put his finger on the car horn and held it there as he edged forward. The thug eventually stood aside and Simon drove into the yard amidst a storm of boos and cat calls.

Once inside the office the clamour could no longer be heard. Bill was at his desk seemingly immune to the hostile mob. 'We've called the police,' he said barely looking up. 'So sorry you were caught by that mob. They tried to come right up to the building here but our guys all came out, looked threatening and the Nazis retreated.'

'They're bloody brain dead,' said Peter Seldon. 'Seems they were around the town earlier. Police had to stop them throwing stones at the

synagogue windows.'

'That's why I called them Nazis,' said Bill. 'According to Fircomb, I and my like were all shipped into this nation by Jews hoping to destabilise us.'

Simon grinned. 'Bill, you are the epitome of stability.'

Peter laughed. 'Epitome, that's a funny word for a Yorkie to use.'

Simon laughed now. 'I could use a much shorter one.'

School term was still over a month away. Simon and Angie shared time seeing the kids were happy and safe. Angie had had an interview with the local hospital for an admin job and been accepted. This would boost the family income but they would have to find some safe haven for the children when both parents were out working.

'We can always ask the Sisterhood,' Simon laughed.

'Oh yes, husband dear,' Angie smirked, 'reckon they would kill and eat Mark and then brainwash Lizzie.'

'I think they're likely vegetarians. Doesn't mean they wouldn't cut the poor little boys balls off.'

Life in the village of Shinkley Green was slow but also strangely satisfying. Simon and Angie, with Mark, had met Mrs Hanbury, the head teacher of the village school and been shown around. They were impressed. The building was modern with a large extension and light and airy classrooms and above all a spacious playground plus a little football pitch. This was a million miles away from the huts and bare facilities of the army. Angie had joined the local Women's Institute and had a warm welcome. Their connection with the popular Bill Gladstone had helped pave the way throughout the village.

'Bill's a lovely gentleman,' said the WI chair. 'He gave us a talk on wartime farming. Some of our members were landgirls and it was so nostalgic.'

One Saturday, a month since the family had settled in Shinkley, they all went by car to a dog rescue centre a mile from the village. Now for the first time they could chose a pet to delight the whole family. They would not be able to bring home any dog they chose that day. There would be a visit to their home by the RSPCA and much paper work to fill in. This was clearly right and proper. The children had fallen in love with an ageing Labrador cross, an affectionate creature that had licked the youngsters' faces. The odd moment was on the journey home. Simon took what he thought might be a short cut down a narrow back lane in open country. It was so similar to a route

he had taken several times on farm visits but this time he was wrong. They rounded a corner and there on the right hand side was a driveway with heavy ten foot high metal gates. On either side of these were flag poles. One flew a union flag and the other an odd banner that seemed to show a lion gripping a lightening bolt. Two muscular, sinister thugs standing guard carried baseball bats and behind them a sign board revealed this place to be the national Head Quarters of the BPP. Simon rapidly drove onwards and was relieved to reach the main road for Shinkley. He and Angie glanced at each other but said nothing. The children continued happily chattering in the back.

That evening was the Kellinghams' turn to come to dinner. This unusual family had rapidly become their friends. The unruly Kellingham children played with Mark and Lizzie and neither of the latter seemed in any way contaminated by their new companions' lack of discipline. The family loved their new home and the village of Shinkley, though it had its eccentric side. Over dinner they told Hugh and Christine about their day and the sight of the BPP house.

'I've never met this Fircomb,' said Hugh. 'The BPP are building support in London but mostly in the areas that used to support Mosley in the 1930s. Nobody here much likes them.'

'I was caught up in one of their demos when they tried to invade the Gladstone yard,' said Simon.

'Yes, that was reported in the local press. But they've had it in for Bill for a while.'

Simon nodded. 'We heard they'd been attacking the synagogue in the town.'

'Yes, the police drove them off so they moved to Bill's place. Then they daubed a church hall on the outskirts of town – seems the Muslim community hires it for prayers on Fridays.'

They all sat down to dinner and Angie served a delicious roast pork joint with all the trimmings and a vegetarian roast for Cassandra. Simon opened some bottles of wine from one of the new established local vineyards. To everyone's surprise it was good. They moved into the sitting room for coffee and talk. No politics thank goodness but they spoke of music that both Simon and the others enjoyed. Then they went outside to see the Kellingham clan pack into their shiny Jaguar and depart with waves and loud goodbyes.

They both waved in return and Angie spoke. 'I met the minister of our local Methodist chapel. He's invited us to their services.'

'All right,' said Simon. 'I've never been that religious; only that

time we were under fire in Cyprus. I prayed a lot then.'

'Well,' Angie replied. 'I think it would be nice if we went as a family to church sometimes.'

'Yes, all right. It would give us an air of respectability. I don't know if the Kellinghams go in for church.'

Angie laughed. 'That I would doubt.'

'Are their kids leading ours into bad ideas? I mean all this talk about free will and relevant awareness?'

'No ours are behaving themselves. Lizzie told me in these really hot days the Kellingham kids run around their garden naked. It doesn't worry me too much but our two were squeamish and refused to join them.'

'I should hope not. Trouble is it is so much hotter in summer here than in Yorkshire.'

CHAPTER 9

'Bill's offered me a company car – a spanking new Rover. I get it next week so the Anglia's yours for shopping and school run.' Simon was feeling pleased because Bill Gladstone was pleased with him. He had sold one more high power tractor leaving just one left in the yard.

'Hey,' Angie laughed. 'You can do a few school runs as well, you know. Men do these things down south.'

That was true of course. In Yorkshire there was a demarcation between male and female roles. Simon had already learned that in these parts things were more relaxed.

'Well, Bill says you can't drive the new motor, it's in my name only.'

'Yes, he's fairly traditional. I met his wife, Sarah today, she invited me to coffee. They live in a very swanky house on the edge of town.'

'Angie, love, you are honoured. I've heard about his wife and kids but haven't seen a sign of them at the office.'

'Sarah's nice. You know she's white and posh-speak but still nice. They've two youngsters both exactly the age of ours. They'd make good friends.'

'A bit better behaved than Hugh and Chris's lot?'

'Yes,' said Angie, 'For certain I would guess. She told me about Bill's background. His grandfather was the one from Africa. He bucked the prejudice and built a rich import business. His son, Bill's dad, was the one who moved into engineering. He sent Bill to expensive public school and university but Bill wanted to be in the farm business and he's expanded it. They own a twin dealership somewhere up country near Brum.'

'Yes,' replied Simon. 'They told me about it and I'm due to pay an overnight visit there, if that's Ok with you of course.'

Angie giggled. 'No bed sharing with Brummie maidens.'

'I'll be too busy I guess anyway.'

Mark and Lizzie were exploring. They were following the wide bridleway into the woods. The woods were dark and the overhead foliage blocked out much of the warm sun. They could hear the call of the pigeons overhead and see the odd rabbit scuttle across the path.

This was a new world for them. Back home in Yorkshire on their granddad's farm was a world of rolling dales and open country. So had been their last army house near Salisbury Plain. This woodland place was exciting and new. Their imaginations took hold and they began to see ghosts in the thickets and maybe not all of them were imaginary.

Lizzie grabbed her brother's arm. 'Someone's following us,' she whispered.

'How d'you know?' asked Mark and he sounded nervous.

'I heard them, listen! There it goes again.' They both heard it now the snap of a broken twig somewhere in the gloom behind them. They had both been warned many times never to speak to strangers. Several teachers over the years had warned them about people called *dirty old men* or DOMS. The teachers had never amplified the warnings but lately the young teenage Lizzie had learned the real danger. She pulled Mark into a thicket of brambles and ash saplings and had covered his mouth with her hand when he tried to yelp from a scratch. They waited and then they saw her: a little girl hardly more than twelve-years-old and wearing the oddest dress, full length and black with a printed decoration of roses. Lizzie restrained a giggle and then called out. 'Hi there.'

The girl stopped and jerked her head in their direction. Well in spite of her odd clothes this was not the ghost of some Victorian tragic heroine. Lizzie and Mark left their hideaway and came back onto the pathway. 'Who are you?' said Lizzie and why were you following us?'

'I'm Freedom,' said the girl. 'That's what they call me, but I'm not free. It's just that I've seen you around and you're happy. I wanted to talk to you.'

Following this odd statement Lizzie looked closer. The girl was tiny. Her odd gown was clean but her feet were bare and filthy. 'I'm Elizabeth and this is my brother, Mark. We've not long moved here, but who are you and are you local?'

'I live in Shinkley like you do,' she replied. 'But I'm not happy. I lost my mum and dad and then they sent me to my auntie and she's horrible.' She dropped her voice. 'I hate her. She won't let me play with other children and she killed my little cat.'

'Killed your cat?' Lizzie was horrified and Mark gasped.

'Little, Nobby, I loved him...' The girl sobbed now and Lizzie threw her arms around her. 'My aunt said he was a man cat and she hated him for it,' she sobbed for some thirty seconds. 'Then Nobby

was sick on her desk. So…so, no I can't say…'

'No, said Lizzie. 'Don't; you are coming home with us.'

'Look after this girl. I'm on my way to the police now!' Simon called.

Angie had never seen him in this state. The children had come home with this ragged child in tow. Clearly the little girl was the subject of abuse but what sort of abuse was not clear. Angie had led little Freedom into the sitting room and given her an orange drink.

Very slowly the child had told her whole story. Freedom was not her real name. It was the one imposed on her by the Shinkley sisterhood. The child had lost both parents in an air disaster. Her aunt, the same Shartcroft who had sworn at Simon, had started on a course of brain washing and it hadn't worked. Freedom still remembered who she was for real and resented the ideological pressure. She rebelled and refused to accept the teaching of her carers. She wanted to mix with other children and go to the village school. Angie had found herself crying at the final revelation. The one thing that Freedom kept from her former life was her cat. One day Shartcroft had taken the creature and Freedom had been forced to watch the cruel murder of her pet. That was enough for Angie and Simon. This was a matter for the law. Freedom was given a hot bath and some fresh clothes although she still refused the offer of shoes.

'You two, look after your new friend and she's not to leave the house.' Angie called.

She went into the village street and walked the short distance to the Kellingham house.

'Chris, you're a magistrate. I want advice.' Angie had found Christine Kellingham at home and at once plunged into the story of little Freedom.

'Well, this isn't entirely new information,' said Christine. 'There's been rumours flying around but every time social services call at that house they get no co-operation only abuse.'

'Surely they shouldn't just walk away.'

'No choice I'm afraid – couldn't do a thing without a writ and it does seem that Ms Shartcroft has some sort of legal guardianship. But the little girl has broken out of this jail more than once and the locals have begun to talk.'

'If we can prove about the poor cat,' Angie was becoming angry.

'Yes, if we can secure proof, that will mean a criminal charge and there would be grounds to remove the child. But it will be proof that we need.'

'Then I'll bloody well get it.'

'Tell you what we could try,' said Christine. 'Try Sally Lederman at the local rag. She's had a watching brief on the sisterhood.'

Angie gratefully accepted a strong drink. Then she walked home.

Simon arrived home an hour later. 'Social services are going to visit the witches and find out what they know. Then another lot are going to talk to the poor little kid.' He threw himself down in an armchair. 'We're to look after the young'un until they come. Where is she?'

'She's upstairs playing with our two,' said Angie. 'They seem to be getting on well.'

'Does she know what her real name is? It can't be Freedom.'

'I don't know what she's told our kids but she may not know after all that brainwashing.'

'I wanted to go straight up there and give the witches a piece of my mind but the police said I could be in trouble as well and I can't let this damage my job.'

CHAPTER 10

The following morning a car pulled into the drive and two women from social services knocked on the front door. Freedom had spent the night on a camp bed in Lizzie's room although later she had crawled tearfully into the older girl's bed and then slept soundly.

Earlier Simon had left for work and only Angie and the three children remained in the house.

'The young lady is Anna Goodhouse.' The social worker began. 'She is officially fostered by her aunt who is Erica Shartcroft who now calls herself Progress Shartcroft. We called on Ms Shartcroft half an hour ago and she refused to speak with us except to say she repudiated the fostering and the child is our responsibility.'

'May we speak to her?' asked the second social worker.

'Lizzie, go and fetch her,' said Angie.

Lizzie reappeared with Freedom, or Anna as she must now be known. The little girl, and she really was very slight in build, was dressed in an oversize pair of Mark's best trousers and a summer blouse of Lizzie's. She still walked barefoot.

At the request of the social workers the child went with them into the lounge for a private talk. Lizzie pulled at her mother's elbow. 'Mum, Freedom wants to stay with us, she told me just now. She's scared those people will take her back to the woman who killed her cat.'

Angie was uncertain. She was desperately sorry for this poor abused kid, but she wasn't sure about committing her own beloved family to caring for a traumatised youngster. Her anger was simmering as she thought of that awful crone murdering a little girl's beloved pet. Simon had called at the town police station and had a somewhat cynical reception. He had assumed no action would be taken and Angie was surprised to see outside a second car, a police car. Then two officers one male one female had knocked on the door.

'We believe you have a certain young child staying with you,' said the male officer.

Angie didn't like the man's tone and she reacted. 'She's been ill treated and she ran to us for help. We've two ladies talking to her right now. Sorry, but you'll have to wait until they're finished.'

The woman PC smiled now. 'It's allright, Mrs Robsby. Nobody's accusing you of anything. But we need to regularise an unusual situation.'

'As long as you don't frighten the poor little girl, she's suffered enough.'

The social workers came out of the lounge followed by Anna who then followed Lizzie and Mark upstairs. Then with the police and Angie all the adults sat down at the dining room table while Angie filled in reams of official forms. The Robsby family were assigned official foster care of Anna for a period of a month with the case being reviewed later. 'We'll keep in daily touch with you – and now the police?' the social worker looked at the two officers.

'The ladies who call themselves the Shinkley Sisterhood are not liked in their village. We understood the child in question has absconded before. We will investigate the case of animal cruelty and if evidence emerges there will be a prosecution...'

A social worker intervened. 'We will be seriously considering a prosecution for cruelty and neglect and the child would then be able to testify about the loss of her pet cat.'

Well the die was cast. Angie saw the police and social workers to their cars and went back indoors. She called upstairs and the three children came down.

'Anna,' Angie smiled,' you will be living with us for a month. How do you feel?'

'I want to stay with you. I won't go back to those women. I hate them – they're bad.'

'She wants to go to school in the village with Mark,' said Lizzie.

Angie was not sure. This was all too complicated and how would Simon react when he came home and found this new, however temporary, family member? In fact Angie had reckoned without her husband's sense of duty. He had returned home from work and Angie had raced out to meet him. Her apprehension dissolved as her man hugged and kissed her. 'You've done the right thing, love and now I'd like to meet our new guest myself.'

Anna had spoken little to either Angie or the children since the police and the others had left. It was strange that the little girl took to Simon at once. She was all smiles as he shook her hand with his best fatherly manner. She burst into a stream of chatter. Now they learned that her dad and mum had died in an air crash. The father had been an airline pilot and her American-born mother a stewardess and both had died in a crash caused by turbulent weather over a mountainous

region. 'That's why I was sent to that horrible aunt. Mum had told me about her and how she hated men and would never forgive mum for marrying a man and 'cos he came from the Isle of Man that made it worse and she needed to beat it out of me. Oh, I hate her, I hate her!'

Simon glanced at Angie and pulled a wry face. He knew that the Sisterhood were by reputation delusional but this was insanity. He pulled his wife aside and beckoned her to leave the room with him. 'That's a great little kid and you've done the right thing taking her in. I went to see the local rag today and their reporter told me the trouble with these women is really only the leader Shartcroft. The other two girls in there are scared of her. She's domineering. The others want to campaign on women's issues but Shartcroft is a fanatic. She hates all men.'

Angie dabbed a tear. 'Oh Simon, just as we've found this lovely house we have all this trouble.'

'No, love. Life's not that easy. Things happen and we'll do our best.'

CHAPTER 11

The children and Anna spent another peaceful night and Simon left for work as usual. They had heard not a word from either police or social services. Angie said she would drive Anna into town and buy some better clothes. They could do nothing about applying to the village school until they heard from officialdom. Simon had made sure he would be on time at the office. This was his military training cutting in. It was odd that the others sensed all was not well and Simon was forced to tell them the whole story.

'Why do all these crazy people settle in Shinkley?' asked Bill.

Simon grinned. 'What about me?'

'Well, just don't let the aura infect you. You're too important to us.'

'I hope it's all right, but I told the authorities to contact me here if anything resolves today.'

Peter Seldon frowned. 'I'm not against women running things if they want to. My missus holds down a good job at the council. But that Shartcroft bitch wants to exterminate men. How does she expect the human race to produce babies?'

'Yes,' said Bill. 'See what I meant about Shinkley. Shartcroft wants to eliminate men and the BPP want another holocaust. With those two around what chance has a black man.'

'Yes,' Peter roared with laughter. 'And if Lady R-L bans sex what chance then?'

'I gather,' said Bill. 'She says that you mustn't do it on Sunday and if you do it in the week you mustn't enjoy it.'

'We may live in Shinkley,' said Simon. 'But we don't buy that.'

'Then there's always old Blabbermouth,' said Peter. 'He told the Sisterhood that women were chattels, possessions of men. Then they came back a week later with a screeching mob and tried to ransack his mansion.'

'That's Shinkley,' said Bill.

Simon was relieved to be back on the road again. This time he had a call some thirty miles to the north in Hampshire. He had the satisfaction of selling the third of the high power tractors to a farm

contractor near Alton. This earned him a nice lunch in the Swan Hotel in that town's high street. Afterwards he found a phone box and called home. Angie reported that she had bought Anna a full outfit but had heard nothing from authority. An hour later he sold a range of lawn mowers to a garden centre. He didn't want to be conceited but it seemed he was good at this job. In this his Yorkshire speech was a big plus. Blunt it could be but it seemed to these southerners it meant honesty.

'We've had a call from your old commanding officer,' said Angie. 'Seems the police have been checking up on you and he told them you were a sober citizen and never a menace to young girls.'

Simon was shocked. He'd never expected this.

'Yes,' said Angie. 'I didn't mention the girl in Gladstone's office.'

'What girl in the office?'

'Oh, don't get all het up. I trust you. It was Sarah Gladstone that time I had tea at her house. Don't worry we laughed.'

'Oh, it's that girl Sharon in reception. Well, she only eighteen and about as daft as they come.' Simon was still worried. The colonel knew all about Melina in Cyprus and Angie most certainly did not. Well, Melina had been twenty something and definitely legal.

At that point all three children burst into the room. Little Anna looked transformed in grey skirt and white blouse. For some reason she still refused to wear shoes. She ran to Simon and tugged at his sleeve. 'Show me your garden – please.' Then she ran outside.

Lizzie was giggling. 'Dad, you're a man. You see the chief witch told her to hate all men. It didn't work; it's me and mum she's wary of. She likes Mark though he's not a man yet.'

Hugh Kellingham called an hour later. 'You know Chris is a magistrate? Well, we've just heard that Shartcroft has been arrested and charged with child abuse and animal cruelty. She's been bailed, but watch out. She doesn't know the little girl is with you but people around here talk.'

CHAPTER 12

The next week was relatively peaceful. They learned that Shartcroft was to appear before the town magistrates in ten days time and more than likely she would be tried by a higher court. It was strange how reconciled the family were to their new member. Anna was a quiet child who ate her meals played in the garden and caused no aggravation. The family's two children seemed to adore her and kept asking if she could stay for ever. That decision was in the hands of a family court. Apart from the Shartcroft the authorities had found no blood relations for the little girl so fostering was inevitable. Then they had a pleasant surprise. The RSPCA called for a second time and with them came the family's new pet the ageing Labrador, named Lonny. All the children loved this new arrival and petted and brushed him and insisted on feeding him. Anna still mourned for her dead cat but Lonny was great therapy for the child and now she smiled for the first time since she joined the family.

It was one Saturday, a fine day with a warm sun. Simon had just finished mowing the lawn when a car drove up the drive. Two women emerged and walked to the front door. They did not look like council officials or salespersons. They were both dressed in fashion jeans, off shoulder sun tops and sandals. 'I'm Tessa,' said the first one and this is my colleague Stefanie. We're representing the Women's Liberation movement of the UK. May we talk?'

'I suppose so,' said Simon in a none too friendly tone, 'but you can't take little Anna. She's still legally in our care.'

'No, we're here to clear the air. The child has been scandalously treated and, please, this sort of thing is not us – not what we're about.'

'No,' said the woman called Stefanie. She was pretty and spoke with a slight American accent. 'We both have male partners. We don't hate men. We only want more opportunities for our sex. It's this bloody glass ceiling. Honestly the nation would gain if we had equal number of women MPs and top civil servants.'

'That's right,' said her companion. 'The Shinkley Sisterhood have been a huge embarrassment to us. Our organisation owns the house they've lived in. Ms Shartcroft will not be allowed back there and we are replacing her with moderate and sensible activists.'

'Oh, please come in,' said Angie who had appeared behind him. 'I think it's better you don't see little Anna, but please come in and we'll talk.'

Angie made the guests a pot of tea and then they settled down to discuss the situation.. By now Simon was more relaxed although not wholly free of suspicion. Tessa and Stefanie, as they now were, began to explain. 'We've been to the house,' said Tessa. 'But Ms Shartcroft wasn't there. We believe she needs urgent psychiatric help. The other two girls in the house looked relieved. She's made them adopt silly names. She was called Progress and the other two were Liberty and Peace. She was such a bully that they had to have these names...'

'How daft is that,' said Stefanie.

'Honestly, we're not extreme. We've a member in the local Tory party. Rufus Blanner your MP is standing down at the next election and we were hoping to put forward Jill Hilldown as his replacement. She's Lord Hocklington's daughter...'

'I know her brother,' said Simon. 'Nigel, he runs the estate office. I sold them a tractor.'

'Well, Jill is an aristocrat and a Tory but she's also one of us. So we're not all man hating loonies.'

Simon found his prejudice fading. These girls might be fighting for the unattainable but they were decent people. If they were to move into the sisterhood house then they would be nice sociable neighbours. Simon remembered women soldiers attached to his own company, one of whom would have been wholly capable of commanding men. They said goodbye to these guests and back indoors found their own children lurking in the passage where they had plainly been listening. Little Anna had fled upstairs but joined them once she was sure the visitors had left.

Simon had determined that he would have no truck with either the local or national politics that seemed to wash through life in Shinkley. Then their friend Hugh approached them. 'We're having a live debate in the village hall next week. The government are negotiating for us to join the European Common Market. I'm putting the case for and old Blabbermouth is against. He's defying Ted Heath but he's leaving Parliament and doesn't care.'

'Look, Hugh. I'm a soldier, we're not into politics. This trouble with the Sisterhood has been bad enough.'

Hugh laughed. 'That's all right, Simon. We're not expecting you to join a party. It's just that it might be a bit of fun.'

'No, you should go,' said Angie. 'And you should take Lizzie.

She's old enough to have a taste of politics. I must stay here to look after the other two.'

It was Monday and Simon was back on the road again. It was a mixed morning. He failed to interest an estate near Horsham in a new tractor but then sold a small market garden tractor to a smallholder at Midhurst. The man was an ex-Para and he hinted he'd had connections with Special Forces. It was good that in this area of Southern England to be ex-service of any type was a bond. He left with the dozen fresh free range eggs that the smallholder's wife had given him and gently packed them away in the boot of the Rover.

On the return journey he pulled over into the car park near the summit of Harting Down and ate the sandwiches that Angie had prepared for him. No doubt if Angie had been a women's libber he would have had to make these himself. How lucky he was to have this lovely girl as his wife as well as two intelligent children: three children now. At that moment he resolved to fight for little Anna to join their family and take the name of Robsby. She so clearly loved all of them. They could offer her a real life. Somehow her arrival seemed intended.

Angie was waiting for him. 'Shartcroft is going on trial next week. It's a magistrates hearing and social services say she will likely be sent for trial at Crown Court. The difficult bit is that Anna will have to testify at the main trial but they say she can answer questions from behind a screen. Tell you some more. It seems the police have found some fresh evidence but no one knows just what.'

The village hall was crowded. Simon was surprised at this. Political apathy was the mood of the time but in this case it seemed the village sensed some real life entertainment very different from the Television. The stage was set with a table and three chairs. Then the contestants walked on stage. Rufus Blanner was greeted with applause and a rather ironic cheer. Then Hugh Kellingham walked on to a warm welcome. The man was clearly popular and deserved to be. Simon didn't know the chairman although he was told the man was a local doctor and therefore considered neutral. He glanced at Lizzie sitting beside him. She looked bored amongst this middle-aged company and he couldn't really blame her. The chair called for quiet and Hugh stood up and put the case for joining the European Common Market. It was a well spoken and coherent case and Simon felt half convinced. A small thirty-something aged man stood up in the audience. He wore

44

a leather jacket and sported a crewcut head. Simon had seen this man before or at least pictures of him.

'Yes, Mr Fircomb,' said the chair.

'We've missed out you fools,' yelled Fircomb. So, this was the BPP's national leader. 'We had a united Europe in 1940 with a great leader. Why did we reject this and then plunge our Europe into five years of pointless slaughter and then let Stalin's red Russian scum take over so much of our Eastern lands.'

Simon was pleased to hear the roar of disapproval from the whole hall. Lizzie beside him was fully awake now. 'Dad, does that man really love Hitler?'

Simon felt angry himself now. He remembered his Uncle Sam who had died fighting just after D-Day and his own wounded father, and then there was the local Lederman family. Jewish – what chance would they have stood let alone poor Bill Gladstone?

Fircomb having said his piece stalked out of the hall to a chorus of boos. Rufus Blanner was grinning and Hugh had a smile.

'Mr Blanner,' said the chair.

Rufus Blanner rose. His face seemed an extra shade redder. He reached inside his jacket and withdrew a line of jangling war medals. 'This is the Military Cross, the MC. I spent four years in the trenches of the Great War. I saw friends die. My only brother died. Why were we there – why? We were there to save the French from the Germans. Don't get me wrong. The Germans are wrong'uns, still are and always will be. The French were our enemies for centuries. Then they call us to save them. Well we do it twice and then that man De Gaulle says we're an inferior nation and he doesn't need us in his new empire. We're trying to join his empire now he's gone and who is pushing us – who? It's the Yanks and the CIA. Do you remember King Henry Fifth. How would our great William Shakespeare sum up today...' Blanner puffed out his chest and orated.

'The Eytie the Dago
The Froggie and the Kraut
We all hate you
Stay out – out – out!'

Blanner sat down to warm applause from a section of the audience.

'Mr Kellingham,' said the chair. 'I'm sure you would like to reply to that.'

Hugh was on his feet. 'The Germans are not bad people but they

have been horribly misled. Mr Fircomb, who grieves for Mr Hitler has a warped view of Europe. Hitler would never have allowed our industries and crafts to rival his. His own cruel united Europe would have taken everything and given nothing but bloodshed and repression. Germany today has embraced true democracy. We trade with her on equal terms. How much more trade would we win as part of a united continent. We have fought two wars with the French on our side. General De Gaulle is not speaking for France. We offered him refuge and he repays us with disdain. It is no good Mr Blanner bringing up King Henry the Fifth. In those days we were so often the invaders ourselves.' Hugh sat down also to a round of applause.

A tall woman was standing eyeing the platform 'Yes Mrs Hilldown,' said the chair.

The woman spoke with that self-confident cut glass voice that automatically raised Simon's north-country hackles. 'I am so sorry to clash with a respected colleague but Rufus Blanner, as you will all know, is not in line with his party. Mr Heath our Prime Minister is negotiating a treaty that will bring new wealth and security to ourselves and all our neighbours and we think that is better than fighting wars.'

Simon knew he had heard of this woman but in what context he was pushed to remember. There were a few more questions asked and then a show of hands taken which split the meeting evenly but by a few votes in favour of Hugh's pro entry. It was all very nice and democratic apart from the unpleasant rant of the deluded Wallace Fircomb.

They left the hall all shading their eyes as they met the bright sunlight. 'Well, Lizzie, what did you make of all that?'

'Not much,' she replied. 'I didn't take to that grumpy old MP and that Nazi is evil, but Hugh did Ok. But the woman who spoke up at the end is the one those women's libbers they were talking about. I know I shouldnt've been listening but they were loud.'

'Who is she then?'

'She's the odd one. A Tory women's libber; that doesn't sound right does it?'

Yes, now he remembered she was Lord Hocklington's daughter and maybe a future MP. This bloody politics was all beyond him. In that way he remained a soldier.

CHAPTER 13

'We've had another visit by social services,' said Angie.

Simon had just returned home from work and was anxious to get in a shower and have a drink. 'What did they say?'

'It's good news. Our situation is unusual but they are going to support our application to foster Anna.'

Simon gave his wife a hug. 'That's great news.'

'It gets better. They say we can register her with the village school.'

'We'll have to get a move on. There's only eight days to go to their autumn term.'

Simon ran upstairs and dived into the bathroom. Ten minutes under the shower was a relief from a hard and sweaty day's work. He still couldn't sell this final high power tractor that remained in the Gladstone yard. One plus, when he returned to the office he found Sharon slobbering over a photograph of her new man, a young farmer from somewhere over Crawley way. Bill had given him another bonus and he and Angie were invited to dinner with Bill and his family.

The next morning Angie had a phone call from Christine Kellingham. She said that Erica (Progress) Shartcroft had been before magistrates and had been sent for trial in the crown court. That trial would not be for at least a month and in the meantime Shartcroft had been bailed but ordered to live more than ten miles from Shinkley. Poor little Anna would have to testify but Christine said the girl would give her evidence from behind a screen.

Simon had spent the day in the office immersed in paperwork, telephone calls and fax messages. Bill and Peter both congratulated him on his sales performance and it was this evening that Angie and he were due at Bill and Shelia's for dinner. That meant all three kids would be parked on the Kellinghams for the evening. He could only hope that none of the Kellingham children's supposed free spirits would contaminate them. Lizzie had promised to keep a close eye on Anna and not to join in any naked frolics with those others. Yes, free expression and relevant awareness. Not for his kids!

The Gladstone family lived in a Victorian style house in a leafy street

47

to the north of the town. It was stylish and detached in a large well-maintained garden. Angie had already taken tea there with the family and on that occasion she had been accompanied by her own children. Sarah Gladstone was a plump fair-haired woman who appeared still dressed in overalls and gardening gloves. They were introduced to the two children, a boy, Harry, aged ten and an elder sister, Charlotte sixteen. The children were mixed race of course and Charlotte in particular was set to be a real beauty. They were polite and well spoken; a huge contrast to the three Kellinghams. No relevant awareness here thank God, thought Simon. He could make soldiers of these two.

The house was so sumptuous that Simon half expected to see domestics, but no, Sarah and Charlotte vanished into the kitchen while Bill poured them a superb dry sherry that slipped over the tongue like nectar. The meal served was also a delight: a tasty vegetable soup was followed by the roast pork joint which Bill carved with one of those new electric gadgets. Yes, no vegetarian option here. Simon had asked him not to talk shop at the meal but the conversation swung onto discrimination. 'That mad Shinkley woman has done no end of damage to our women's cause,' said Sarah. 'It affects Bill and me and others. We like playing golf but we have to drive nearly thirty miles to get a game,'

'Really,' Simon didn't know what to say.

'Oh yes, the nearest course and club is just north of here. But I can't join because women are banned at weekends, Bill can't join because he's black and the Ledermans can't because they're Jews.'

Bill laughed. 'Rufus Blanner is the club chairman and if you want to join, Simon, you'll have to stand on the carpet in front of his committee and prove you're a fit and proper person.'

'No thanks,' said Simon. 'So where do you play?'

'We have to drive all the way to a course near Eastbourne. They're a bit snobbish but they like us.'

'So they bloody should,' said Sarah. 'Bill stumped up half the cash for their new pavilion.'

'Sorry but neither of us are into golf,' said Simon.

'Ever done any sailing?' asked Sarah.

'Oh yes. While I was based in Cyprus we had a little mini-yacht club. We had a lot of fun racing Royal Navy Fourteen footers. It was a relief from foot patrols and being shot at.'

Both their hosts looked delighted. 'Good,' said Bill. 'We've got a slightly bigger boat in the marina across the way. She's a Contessa 32.

We race her at Cowes and we've crossed the channel a couple of times. How do you fancy a sail in her?'

'What about it, Angie?' Simon felt excited.

'Well, I haven't done much more than muck about in a kayak. But I'd be keen to give it a go. Thanks, Bill.'

'I'll let you know,' Bill looked pleased. 'Can't take Peter from work, even in a flat calm he always says he feels seasick. You've missed Cowes this year but why not come along for Round the Island next June? That's a race with a few hundred boats but it's really just for fun.'

'Yes, I've heard of it. Bill we'd be delighted.'

'We'll see if we can give you a bit of a run out before we lay up in October. Bring your kids, we'll bring our kids and it'll be great fun.'

It was time to take coffee in the lovely high-ceiling drawing room. The Gladstones had a television with one of these new video recorders. They had set this to record the local news on Southern TV. It was the one gloomy moment when the third story in was a report of the Shartcroft committal. The whole family worried about this. Social services said they must in no way coach Anna before she gave evidence but a sympathetic prosecution person would chat to her and her foster parents could be with her at the trial. Anyway there were still over three weeks until the hearing.

They said goodnight to the Gladstone family and invited them to a return dinner in Shinkley. Simon felt so lucky at having landed a secure employment with such a good boss and a whole team of great people.

Time was certainly flying by. The village school had suggested Mark and Anna attend an introductory session a day before the term started officially. Lizzie was to be pitched into the town comprehensive on day one. The girl was confident she could stand up for herself. Simon was satisfied that his daughter's military background would pay dividends and she would not be intimidated by these Southern kids. Then a great day. At a farm just over the Kent border he sold the final high power tractor. The farmer was a retired Guards sergeant and the two of them had reminisced about their times in Cyprus and Germany.

All reservations the family had about Anna had vanished. They had accepted her and she accepted them with joy. The other children told them that Anna still felt sadness for the loss of her true parents but had only memories. She loved playing music but the Shartcroft woman had murdered her beloved cat and destroyed her violin. Her toys must

have been dispersed by the sale of her parent's house. These memories would never leave her and she suffered occasional nightmares, but she was grateful to have found a loving family and a safe refuge.

The day came when Simon drove to collect Lizzie from her new school at the end of her first day. The younger children were allowed to walk the few hundred yards from the village school to home. Lizzie had a face lit by an excited smile.

'Well how did you get on?' he asked.

'Oh, dad. I'm going to like it here. I know I will. They tested me and I'm in a group ready for O Level GCE. It used to be an all girls school but they've let boys in now and I've met a lovely one. He's called Gareth and he's in their junior rugby team – so what about that?'

'As long as your mother and I approve of this Gareth I suppose there's no harm.' Simon was less than sure about this. He didn't want his daughter chasing boys and even if her choice was harmless it would divert her from study.

Lizzie was jumping up and down. 'Our maths teacher is Mrs Sotherington. And wow, we did a preliminary test for her and I was first out of twenty.'

'That's more like it,' her father was really pleased now. 'Work at those studies and don't get too tied up with boys.'

Lizzie sniggered. 'Oh, Dad, I don't think Gareth is into tying up girls. He's ever so gentle.'

Simon at this point gave up. He would discuss the situation with the girl's mother back home.

CHAPTER 14

This was now the day they had been dreading. The Shartcroft trial was due with Anna as a key prosecution witness. They had been visited by a nice and sympathetic police woman who had spoken gently to Anna. She was to answer all the questions truthfully and not to add or embroider anything.

The crown court selected was not held in their neighbouring town but in another some miles away. Angie had dressed Anna in her smartest new clothes and persuaded her to put on a nice pair of black slip-on shoes. An hour before they were due to start the house received a call from social services. They gave exact directions and parking advice for the court house and then. 'We've arranged for Anna to enter the building through the rear entrance. We understand that there is a noisy demonstration in the street outside the front door.'

The journey took an hour. The atmosphere was tense and Anna sat in the back of the Rover and spoke not a word throughout the journey. They arrived and showed a pass that allowed them to use the exclusive car park at the rear of the building. They were greeted by two more social services ladies whom they did not know and Anna was whisked through the rear door of the court.

An odd wailing sound was filtering around the corner of the building from the street in front. Angie and Simon walked round to the front entrance. Lined along the street being watched by police was a gathering of some twenty women waving placards.

Release the Shinkley One – No Stitch Up – Justice For Women – No Man Court.

Suddenly the throng began to sing. Simon stopped short and Angie nearly bumped into him. Both were startled. The tune was a hymn that both had sung in Methodist chapels. John Bunyan's *To be a Pilgrim.* But these words were different.

She who would a feminist be
Let her come hither
Organise collectively
Come wind come weather
No Male discrimination

Shall halt her determination
Through march and demonstration
To be a feminist.

The song ended and the mob began a fresh round of chants and banner waving.

Inside the building Simon and Angie were shown to a waiting room before their case was heard. The place was gloomy and reminded Simon of a mainline railway station.

Eventually after what seemed an eternity a male usher escorted them to the gallery. They looked down into a courtroom. The bench was empty but in the well of the court people were bustling around including bewigged lawyers and, oddly, a man pushing a trolley. On it was a battered metal cabinet with a glass door. Simon had seen something of its likes before in the officers mess kitchen. The jury began to file into their box and shortly afterwards all rose as the judge entered. Lastly the accused was led into the dock by two female officers. Shartcroft looked arrogant and assured.

Now it was the time for the prosecution to open their case. The barrister was a man and Simon saw Shartcroft glare with a look of real hate. The case opened with details of Anna's fostering. Then: 'this child was subjected to what is commonly called brainwashing. She was told to forget her real parents and to adopt a very extreme code of feminist World domination. This child has spirit and resisted all indoctrination. She ran away three times and twice was forcibly returned to the commune. But social services officers were now alert and were alarmed. They called officially at the Shinkley commune but were refused access to the child.

'Your Honour. I have only two witnesses and first I would like to call Miss Anna Goodhouse. The young lady has been identified by the court but in view of the delicacy of the case she will give her evidence from behind this screen.' The barrister pointed to the folding screen at a corner of the room but within view of the lawyers and the bench. Simon and Angie leant forward but could see no sign of Anna.

'Miss Anna,' said the barrister. 'Were you at any time happy in Ms Shartcroft's house?'

Anna's soft voice replied. 'No, she was horrible. She bullied me and she killed my cat.'

'Very well, we will come to the tragedy of your cat in a moment. Did Ms Shartcroft try to force her ideas on you?

'She told me my dad was evil and my mum shouldn't have married

him and what happened to them both was good. But it's not true. I loved them both. I miss them.'

'Why did you run away?'

'She's my aunt but she's cruel. I wanted to find friends and go to the school and be happy.'

The barrister stood down and now it was the turn of the defence council. 'You're making this up aren't you? Ms Shartcroft offered you a nice home. Why are you so ungrateful?'

'Not true. I know what she did to me. I hate her. She killed my Nobby. He was my cat.'

'You will have to prove that...'

Anna's voice broke in. She sounded shrill and filled with emotion. 'She put poor Nobby in a machine and burned him to death and she made me watch.'

The barrister sounded if not bored then more as a man going through the motions. But Simon was still angry at the man's bullying tone and Angie was beside him dabbing tears. Now the barrister handed back to the prosecutor.

'Call Herbert Cummings.'

Mr Cummings was a grizzled late middle-aged man. He looked uneasy and was dressed in a blue suit. 'Mr Cummings, we understand you are a refuse collector. On the twenty fifth of July you removed a piece of equipment from Shinkley Lodge?'

'Yessir.'

'What was that equipment?'

'It was one o'they new micro cookers. You know them as cooks by electric waves. I took it to the dump and then I reckoned as I could repair and sell it on.'

'Mr Cummings. Is that the one on the trolley here?'

'Yeah, that be the one. And before you asks I marked it before I took it to the law.'

'Can you tell the court how you marked it?'

'Inside o' the door I wrote the date and my job number wi' a marker pen. Then I took it to the law.'

'Why did you do that?'

'Cos' there were a dead body in it. A poor moggy cat what someone had burned to death. Tell you Sir, I saw bad things in the war but this time I were near to being sick.'

The defence council stood. 'No questions, your Honour.'

That's it, thought Simon. He's thrown in the towel. His disgust was rising. He wanted to catch hold of Shartcroft and give her a real

hiding. And there the woman was in the dock, looking oddly pleased.

The judge addressed the defence councillor. 'Are you going to call the defendant?'

'Your Honour, the defendant does not feel she has done anything wrong and has expressed the fact that she does not wish to testify. She also objects to the male gender of the bench and council.'

There was a pause and the judge addressed the jury. He told them, that they would have to take all the evidence seriously and weigh up the testimony on both sides.

Was the child witness malicious? Was the council worker telling the truth? They must examine all this testimony and make a judgement that they all felt was beyond reasonable doubt.

In the entrance hall they met the friendly social worker whom they knew from home. 'Come across the road and have a cup of coffee,' she said. 'I wouldn't expect a verdict for at least an hour and my colleague is going to fetch us when it happens.'

The pro-Shartcroft mob was sitting on the pavement their banners laid out beside them.

'One year with remission will be no more than eight months at most,' said Angie. 'Then what will that old cow do?' They were outside the court in the sunshine waiting to collect Anna for the journey home. The judge had been scathing while passing sentence. "Abuse of small children will not be tolerated. Your offence in cruelly torturing this child's pet cat to death is unimaginable. I only hope that you can receive some psychiatric treatment in prison."

Shartcroft was physically dragged from the dock by two burly police women. She screamed incoherent abuse about men and dire threats to Anna. As the news spread the Shartcroft supporters put up a chant of: '*Men, men – hate – hate – men men – hate – hate.*' Shortly afterwards they dispersed trailing their banners behind them.

Anna ran and flung her arms around both Simon and Angie in turn.

'Come on,' said Simon. 'Let's get out of here and go home.'

The next day they discovered to their horror that the Shartcroft case had been reported in the tabloids and on local television. Then the village of Shinkley had miraculously closed ranks. News reporters had wandered around the village looking for Anna. The reporters had been shunned by the entire village; doors had been shut in their faces and they had been asked to leave the pub. Simon smiled; Shinkley was not such a crazy place after all.

54

CHAPTER 15

Now it was autumn with all three children settled at their schools and seemingly happy and doing well. Lizzie was the intellectual one and already top of her class in maths.

Mark was making friends and Anna, although shy and needing to make up ground with her learning, had sympathetic teachers and with a gift for music was settling in well. Angie was now able to take up her part-time appointment at the hospital. She was happy and the money was useful.

For Simon this was a busy time. On the farms it was end of season a time of post-harvest ploughing and the sowing of winter crops for early harvest next year. He was now becoming familiar with many farms in the area and above all making friends. He was busy selling and delivering spare parts for every sort of farm machine and taking more orders for next year.

The family were beginning to blend into life in Shinkley. The Kellingham family were close friends now. The Shinkley Sisterhood had been dispersed and replaced by two pleasant young women who were adamant in their views but not overbearing. They had issued pamphlets in favour of *Liberation and Free Love*. This had already put them in bad odour with Lady Reece-Lamprey and her League of Decency. Rufus Blanner had announced his resignation from Parliament and would not be standing at the next election. This had put the political associations into a flutter. The BPP had staged another march to the town council offices to protest at allocation of council houses to black and Asian families. The Kellinghams were becoming increasingly excited by all this but Simon was unmoved: he only wanted to keep his head down and get on with his job.

His friend Dan Lederman had told him that Shartcroft was now in a women's open prison somewhere in the Midlands.

Simon yawned. He was sitting in the garden half dozing. Nearby the three children were playing with the substantial metal swing that he had set up. He woke as he heard a voice calling. It was Angie leaning out of the office window waving a telephone handset. 'Love, phone call.'

He walked across to the window. 'It's Mrs Hobbs,' said Angie.

'It's Sunday tomorrow...'

Simon yawned. 'Well I've noticed today is Saturday so Sunday follows. Who is this Mrs Whatsit?'

'She's the minister's wife from the Methodist chapel. They're holding a special children's service and then an adult service in the evening. Can I tell her we'll come?'

'Yes, all right. Can't do any harm.'

Angie withdrew from the window and chattered into the phone. The chapel was at the far end of the village not far from the Kellinghams place. Their friends were openly agnostic, but Simon rather liked the idea of some hymn singing and it would be good for the children.

'What d'you think?' Simon asked the three children.

'Yeah, we'll go,' said Lizzie. 'It'll annoy Cassie. The Kell's don't go much on religion.'

'Anna?'

'Aunt Shart, said churches were all for men. All vicars are men and Jesus was a man. She doesn't like men.'

'I think we gathered that,' said Simon. 'So, do you want a taste of this man's world?'

'Yes, please. We used to go to church and sign hymns when my mum and dad were alive.'

'Right, we'll all go on Sunday.'

The church-going turned out to be a success. Angie had had a struggle to make the children dress soberly; no jeans or lurid tops, and for Anna to wear shoes. Simon had worried this chapel might be a bit in line with those he remembered up north; that meant hell fire, doom and eternal punishment. None of this was heard. The children were exhorted to find the flowers and trees that were symbolic of God's love even though his children on earth were so often greedy and disruptive. In between the preaching and reading the congregation sang hymns. The only sour moment was when they all were invited to sing John Bunyan's *To Be a Pilgrim*. It reminded Simon and Angela of the bowdlerised version they had heard outside the courthouse. Fortunately that time Anna had been inside the court building.

The adult service in the evening had been much the same apart from one surprise. Amongst the congregation was the women's campaigning girl, Stefanie. 'No, I've always been a Methodist from childhood,' she insisted. 'Most of the early suffragettes were Christians,'

56

Stefanie explained that she was now living in the communal house with a small group of fellow campaigners. The Robsby family all liked Stefanie. Originally Simon had assumed she was American until Stefanie explained that she was from British Columbia in Canada.

'That's something good from all this,' said Simon. He looked back and saw that Anna and Mark were ambling some twenty yards behind although Lizzie was with her parents.

'You know,' said Lizzie. 'In Hansel and Gretel the old witch was cooked in her own oven. That'd be fair wouldn't it?'

'No, that's gruesome,' said her mother.

'Apart from anything else,' Simon laughed. 'I can't see the Shartcroft fitting in that tin box. But it's a thought.'

A happy family walked the quarter mile to home. There the children were able to scramble for their casual clothes and Anna to discard her smart shoes.

It was now late September and the family were invited for a trip in Bill Gladstone's yacht before she was laid up for the winter. So on Saturday the family drove the few miles to the Marina on the nearby Harbour. Waiting at the yacht club was the whole Gladstone family. Simon, Angie and the children had never seen anything like this place.

The whole of this little lock-gated lagoon was crowded with every sort of yacht from small family cruisers to magnificent millionaires "gin places". The Gladstone yacht was smart with a bright red hull and she was named *Sea Sprite*. This vessel was not the biggest or in any way the grandest in sight but she was substantial. Bill said she was a design called a *Contessa 32*, one of a number of the same build on this harbour and around the nearby Solent. She was basically a two sail rig: mainsail and a choice of jibs up front and for close quarter manoeuvring she had a powerful auxiliary diesel engine. Once aboard the Gladstone children took charge and showed them all the cabin with its cosy bunks and the galley with its four-burner bottle gas stove. Following the Gladstone family's advice they had all put on extra layers of jumpers and waterproofs. Sarah Gladstone had fitted Anna with a life jacket as well but said her lack of shoes didn't matter. Just after mid day it was high tide and the lock gate was fully open. Bill steered his ship under power out into the harbour and turned West towards the sea. It was a fine warm autumn day with a gentle south-westerly breeze; just right, thought Simon to initiate the family in the joys of sailing. They motored past houses and another yacht club and then the harbour opened up into a wide expanse of glittering sun swept

water.

Bill made no move to hoist sails until they had passed through the Harbour entrance and well out to sea. Then it was all five minutes of frantic action as the Gladstone family heaved on ropes and wound winches. The engine was silenced and they were sailing. It was a moment none of them would ever forget.

'We're working to windward,' said Bill, 'Can't sail straight into the wind but we try and point as near to it as we can. You young lady,' he pointed to Lizzie. 'Take the helm and we're in your hands.' Lizzie smiled nervously and sat down at the tiller.

'You see that funny looking castle over there,' said Bill. 'Steer for that if you can.'

Lizzie took a minute or two to work out that a tiller steer meant pointing a different direction to the one wanted. Once she had mastered this, her eyes shone with delight. Bill explained that they must keep in the deep water channel and be very wary of big ships and the cross-Solent ferries. They all took a turn on the helm and the children mastered the basics and loved it. Simon had sailed before but only in dinghies, and he was delighted at how easily this larger ship handled. They passed the entrance to Portsmouth and then off Cowes Bill turned *Sea Sprite* around and they headed back to harbour. They were now downwind and able to keep a dead straight course. Bill and Sarah set the huge bulging spinnaker and they all watched as the meter in the cockpit read seven knots. An hour later they were back in harbour and shortly afterwards motored up to the lock gate.

There was then a long tedious wait for the gates to shut and the water level to carry them up to the marina. Then they were released and with Sarah at the helm they coasted into their pontoon berth while Bill and Simon secured the lines. It was over and the Robsby family looked at each other eyes shining. Bill put the sails away and then reset an alarm system at the pontoon gate.

'Wish we didn't need that but the harbour security caught some BPP idiots with a can of petrol hovering around. They dropped the can and ran but I guess they were after our lovely boat.'

Simon and Angie glanced at each other. While afloat everything else ashore had faded to nothing, now a sour note had intruded.

'Come on,' said Sarah. 'We've a table booked in the yacht club for dinner.'

Angie smiled at her husband. 'I wish we had a boat like *Sea Sprite*.'

'Win the pools one day and maybe we will.'

'You don't need anything as big,' said Bill. 'I've a neighbour with a little Cadet dinghy for sale. Just right for your three youngsters. Our two have got one already and they'll show yours the tricks.'

CHAPTER 16

It was cold now in mid-November. An icy wind from the Downs to the North blew down on Shinkley. The children were off to school in their winter warmers and Anna had now accepted warm socks and shoes. Simon was grateful for the Rover's powerful heater as he did his rounds of the farms. He made fewer big deals with the large arable farms as all was quiet now with little activity on the land. The smaller farms were different and he did a good trade in milking machines and spares. Simon did not envy the dairy farmers and was glad he had left that life behind when he first joined the army. The family farms worked seven days a week starting at five o'clock every morning. That was a standard of dedication he didn't think he could match.

Shinkley had calmed down these last few months. There was no news of Shartcroft although he understood she had not yet been released from the open prison. As long as the witch made no attempt to settle back in Shinkley he didn't care. Sefanie and her friends were now in possession of Shinkley Lodge to the disapproval of Rufus Blanner who had wound down the window of his chauffeured Bentley and shouted abuse at Stefanie as she walked back from the village shop. Politics still seemed to intrude everywhere in Shinkley. Two canvassers had called from the League of Decency and left a pile of literature. Lady Reece-Lamprey was apparently going to stage a big rally in the town hall to raise the standards of Sussex morality.

'There you are, love,' said Simon. 'No sex on Sunday.'

'Oh, that's sad,' Angie laughed. 'What'll happen if we do?'

'Oh, definitely burn in hell fire.'

'I wonder if our minister and his wife observe that, and what about the local bishop?'

Politics intruded again when Lizzie confided, 'Cassie and Gareth want me to join the Young Liberals.'

Simon was not entirely happy with this. The Young Liberals were run locally by Cassandra Kellingham and they had a national reputation as a wild far-left agitating group. He supposed that was slightly better than the Young Conservative who had the reputation of a well-spoken marriage bureau, or for that matter the Young Farmers who were a mite bucolic. All of these local groups ran social evenings,

dances, and sightseeing trips, so that would at least keep these teenage kids out of most trouble.

'Yes,' said Lizzie. 'Gareth and Cassie want me to go to a concert. It's the Filthy Swine; they're performing in the Town Hall in December.'

Simon knew the Swine were the so-called punk rock group vying to be the most outrageous. Lady R-L's decency rally was due in the same Town Hall this month so maybe these stupid kids should be made to go to that as well. Whatever Lady R-L might say he doubted the Filthy Swine would lead the youngsters into real moral danger.

Soon it would be their first family Christmas away from the army and of course their first in their new home. This would be something really special to be remembered. For poor Anna it would be her first family Christmas since she had lost her parents. Anna had settled in to their lives so well that it seemed she had always been with them. She adored Lonny the ageing Labrador and often she would tempt him to sleep on her cramped bunk bed. Simon smiled; they had all been so lucky. Everything that had happened since he left the service had worked so well for them. It was almost as if all this was somehow meant.

The papers and the Television were full of all this talk about miners' disputes and threatened power failures. Temporarily this was good news as Simon travelled the farms and small businesses selling generators. There would certainly be no "four day week" for him. Hugh and Christine were becoming increasingly excited by the politics involved, but Simon couldn't share any of this. He only wanted to keep his head down and do his job.

He had bought the little Cadet dinghy for the children and it was now stored at the Yacht Club which both he and Angie had joined on a family ticket. The children could hardly wait for the summer to arrive when they could go on a full sailing course on the harbour.

Politics went and intruded again one Wednesday. Simon had pulled into a car park on the Downs Way and saw a motor coach parked nearby. He thought nothing of this as he climbed out and looked for a secluded spot for a pee. On return he was accosted by the coach driver a small man who like the Ancient Mariner called for him to stop and talk. The driver said he was waiting to collect a squad of Marines on a map reading exercise.

'Reckon as them bootnicks is lost,' said the little man. 'I'm a navy man myself.'

'Really, I'm army or was until recently.'

61

The little man looked excited at this and went on to say he was the local organiser for the BPP. 'We're being took over, the Mussies want to make us take their religion and they'll kill all of us if we don't. Yes, on the given day every Muslim man will be told to kill seven Christians...'

Why only seven? thought Simon.

'Yeah, they're taking over. I used to be a Navy man, but did you know there's a Mussie in command of the Channel Navy?'

Simon made no comment, he only wanted to escape from the ancient mariner and eat his lunch. How ignorant or deluded could these BPP be? The Channel Commander he knew was Rear Admiral Hammed and Admiral Hammed was wholly English and from a one hundred year settled family of Anglo Indian Christians.

'I don't really blame the mussies or the coons and pakkies.' said the man. 'It's all a conspiracy by the Yids. Them Jews 'as shipped in all these coloureds to unstabalise the nation. Wallace Fircomb says all the troubles in this world is by scheming yids – why didn't we let Adolf finish the job?'

Simon was tempted to tell the man that he worked for Bill, and was a friend of the Lederman family, but he only wanted to escape from this lunacy. Shortly afterwards the first of the map readers appeared and Simon fled to his car and drove another mile down the road to a nice village pub. He was sorry he'd never told the man that his, Simon's, old C.O, Colonel Cohen was just promoted to brigadier.

CHAPTER 17

Hugh and Christine had come to dinner as they did regularly once a month. Post-meal they had relaxed over coffee in the front room lounge.

'Simon,' Hugh began. 'Next year is our parish council election. Would you let your name go forward?'

This was a shock. 'But Hugh, we've only been here five minutes. Who would take me seriously?'

'Believe me you will be taken very seriously. You've made a huge impression on the village already. You work for Bill and the farmers like you. Above all you were the ones who rescued little Anna and caused the removal of Ms Shartcroft. And you're a no-nonsense former soldier.'

'I still feel a sort of foreigner with a funny accent.'

'Think about it.'

From that point the conversation moved on and Simon privately dismissed the idea. He liked Shinkley but how well did he know its people. It was a more shifting population than say a Yorkshire farming village where there would be very few commuters and where many families were interrelated. He could hear the whine of the front room record player. He excused himself and left the dining room. The kids were playing the Filthy Swine's top twenty disc, with Pete Toilet allegedly singing, although fortunately the words were indecipherable. Anna was squatting in a far corner with Lonny the dog. Lizzie, Mark and Cassie Kellingham were trying to jive without much success amongst the crowded furniture. Simon stared at the youngsters, pulled a disapproving face and went to back to his guests.

The town hall was an impressive building fronted by a Greco-Roman columned arch. In earlier life it had been a corn exchange. Simon and Angie did not know quite why they had been drawn to the LOD rally. Tonight they had left the children in the care of the lady who helped in the house with cleaning. Lady Reece-Lamprey's new morality held no attractions, but it would be interesting to report back to his folks in Yorkshire who were probably more in line with the LOD than they were. A moderate-sized crowd was drifting toward the entrance doors:

all were middle aged or elderly and included a small group of nuns in full habit. Lizzie's Young Liberals had threatened to demonstrate against the rally but this time a universal parental veto seemed to have worked. Not even the Kellingham youngsters had turned out. The BPP were there with placards and leaflets. A leaflet was roughly pushed into Simon's pocket. He glanced at it. Apparently as far as the BPP were concerned Lady Reece-Lamprey was deluded. Falling morals were being orchestrated by Jews and rife among immigrants. No, thought Simon, alcohol and sexual temptation were ingrained into the whole population and he couldn't see Lady R-L turning back that tide.

The hall was impressive and pleasantly warm after the cold wind outside. Rows of red folding seats rose in a sloping tier. In front was a stage with a desk and a microphone. By the advertised start time the hall was about one third full. The ageing audience muttered and some looked curiously at the nuns who were seated three rows in front of their own seats. High up across the top of the stage was a banner. *Let us return to our true traditions.* Or did that mean: bring back Queen Victoria and a sink of drunkenness and ten thousand prostitutes in London alone many of them children. He remembered his grand-mother and aunts remarking that one hundred years before when contraception did not exist, wives were often forced to have a birth a year. After the eighth or even tenth it was easier for the wife to tell the husband to go find relief with a teenage whore. He wondered if Lady R-L knew that.

The lights dimmed and the chair person walked on stage. This was a real shock for the man was Rufus Blanner M.P. Did Lady R-L really not know of the man's lecherous repute? Happily Blanner did not engage in any superfluous blather but immediately called on Lady Reece-Lamprey to take the stage. The lady did not look anything like Simon's perception of a country aristocrat. Lady Reece-Lamprey was a short dumpy late middle-aged woman with a piled up hairstyle. She was dressed as one would expect in a sober dark blue suit only embellished by a bright necklace. Blanner called for silence and next a clergyman dressed entirely in a black robe entered and led the meeting in a long mournful prayer. This called on the audience/congregation to repudiate sins of the flesh and apparently all normal enjoyment.

Lady Reece-Lamprey spoke with a cultivated accent that tended to lapse into a slight midlands tone. Simon had learned that Lady R-L had married a Welsh lord whose estate was here in Sussex. She began. 'In this age of declining moral standards....' Her speech was immediately disrupted. The supposed nuns had stood up, disposed of

64

their habits and began to scream about "free love – for the whole world". Simon was shocked but not wholly surprised that one of the nuns was Stefanie from Shinkley.

'Yes,' Lady R-L yelled into her microphone. 'The devil disguised as a sacred order. Guards remove these vessels of sin and may almighty God reform them and divert them from their path to hell.'

Three surprisingly young and burly security guards dragged the vocal three kicking and screaming from the hall. Simon wondered if these thugs had been hired from the BPP. Lady R-L was now well into her oration. Uncontrolled sex outside marriage was being orchestrated by the corrupt and Satanic-devised rock music. 'All of you must be on the watch for corruption in your own houses and punish severely lapses among your own families...' No good telling the Kellingham family, thought Simon.

'Homosexual perversion is increasing and not been properly punished by the law,' she shouted. 'I look back to happier days when we had the sanction of punishment by rod and rope.'

On cue two couples of men one pair young and the other older had stood up and begun to dance in the isles, arms around each other.

'Police, police!' screamed Lady R-L 'Arrest them – remove them. Charge them!'

This time the intervention came in the enthusiastic form of six uniformed policemen who dragged the demonstrators from the hall to the supportive jeers of most of the audience. Following all this the speaker was left in peace as she ran through a catalogue of perversion and sin including: Television, films and rock music that were 'Corrupting our great nation...' Her voice rose to a crescendo as she denounced; 'That vile man Lawrence has flooded the land with the disgusting filth of his Chatterley book. How could our courts let such a thing happen?' By now Simon only wanted to escape the meeting hall and run. Lady R-L sat down to wild applause from most of the audience and then answered some cleverly planted questions. Rufus Blanner thanked her for her "inspirational speech..." and bid them all good night. What a hypocrite, thought Simon.

Angie turned to him and pulled a wan face. 'Let's go home.'

CHAPTER 18

Simon had agonised for some days. The political dottiness residing in Shinkley Common had really disturbed him. Could he really bring some sanity to the place if he took part in its affairs? Should he accept Hugh Kellingham's suggestion and stand for the parish council. On no account would that be under Hugh's or any other party label. He would be the no-nonsense Yorkshire man bringing some sanity to this corner of the south. He had been told that the parish elections were not to be held until next May and it was now December with Christmas just three weeks away.

But first there was the problem of the children wanting to hear the Filthy Swine perform in the same Town Hall where he had heard Lady-Reece Lamprey. He couldn't think of a bigger contrast. He decided however unpopular it would make him he would accompany the children to this alleged concert. He was also most surprised to be told that Hugh Kellingham was also coming, but in his case he wanted to hear and enjoy the Swine himself. He smiled inwardly maybe Lady R-L would appreciate his concern for the morals of his family. Anyway Christmas was coming and they would make it one in their new home that they would all remember. Above all it must be a landmark family occasion for little Anna.

Two days later and he was on the road north again, this time as a passenger in Bill's Jaguar. They were speeding up the motorway to the Gladstone office in West Bromwich. This was for a meeting of Gladstone sales persons. Simon was surprised at the scope of the Gladstone business that with its associate companies covered most of the UK.

The Birmingham branch was responsible for selling a range of American imported tractors into the grainlands of East Anglia. He was to be away from his family for forty-eight hours. Angie and the youngsters accepted this as Simon had been away so often and longer in his army service days.

Bill drove the Jag with a tenacity that was fast but safe. They had stopped half way for a restaurant meal, not a motorway service station but in a village pub near Tewksbury that Bill knew. Then it happened.

They entered the industrial estate with the Gladstone unit and office. Bill slowed at the last turning when a police car that had been following them for a mile pulled over in front blocking their way. Bill, puzzled wound down his window.

A policeman glared at him. 'You, out and identify yourself.' Simon was angered at the man's tone.

'Why,' said Bill.

'You was driving at thirty eight miles per hour in a thirty mile an hour limit.' The copper paused and glared again. 'That's a posh car for a blackie to drive. You steal it?'

Bill sighed and produced his driving licence. 'I'm not arguing the case with you. That's my licence to drive and if you radio in and check your records you will find this motor car belongs legally to me.' Bill's tone was scathing with an educated public school cadence.

'Sorry, sir, but you got reason to be driving around here?' the policeman had changed his tone but still seemed suspicious.

'Officer, I am on my way to my own company office that is just around the next corner. Gladstone Agricultural Ltd.'

'Yeah, we know it but you don't look like the sort of boss man we know around here. You having me on. I wouldn't try that on me blackie boy.'

Simon had had enough. He opened his passenger side door and climbed out. He was now angry and confrontational. 'Constable, I don't like your attitude. You are insulting an important local employer. I have your numbers and I will make a complaint to your chief constable.' Simon had returned to army days. Once again he was confronting two callow recruits overdue for return to barracks. He held out his own drivers licence. 'I work for this gentleman's company and I can vouch that he is exactly as he has told you.'

The policeman looked slightly chastened and told them that they could go. Simon resumed his seat and he was still angry. 'That man is a bloody disgrace,' he fumed.

'No, leave it,' said Bill. 'It's in their culture. He probably thought he'd nicked a drug dealer. But wait another twenty or thirty years and black-afro professionals like me will be two a penny.'

The incident still riled Simon although he enjoyed the sales conference and the subsequent hospitality as well as the night in a luxury Brum hotel on the edge of the city.

The next morning they made the return to Sussex.

'How did it go?' asked Angie.

'Apart from one incident,' he told her about the police. 'That apart all was fine. The others seem to like me. How was it here?'

'Lizzie and Mark were fine, but little Anna missed you.'

CHAPTER 19

'Oh, Dad, you don't need to watch us. We'll be all right. We'll be with Cassie and her Dad.'

Simon thought that was half the trouble. For some weird reason Hugh Kellingham admired the Filthy Swine and Simon most definitely did not. His army loyalties lay with the monarchy and the Swine's debut single: *Blast the Palace – piss on the Queen* was to him deeply offensive. Punk was the name of this new genre. Simon's popular music tastes ranged from Glen Miller to Elvis. The Filthy Swine were part of the same dottiness that he saw all around him in Shinkley. No, he was going to this event and he was going to keep his children out of trouble and moral contamination. Then inwardly he smiled. Wasn't that exactly what Lady Reece-Lamprey would think? Lizzie and Mark had already walked down the road to the Kellingham house and from there would be on their way to the Town Hall. He would follow shortly. Angie was staying at home with Anna who although musical, thankfully had no taste for the Swine.

A teenage mob was jostling outside the hall and already a van had pulled up and was unloading a speaker system and guitar cases plus a synthesiser. Then the world around went crazy as a Volkswagen camper van drew up with the band members. The four young men looked alarmingly respectable as they were rushed into the stage door away from yelling boys and screaming girls.

'Hi there, Simon, a most interesting evening.' It was Hugh Kellingham dressed in denim and a check shirt. Frankly, thought Simon, they both looked out of place and very old.

'Hello, Hugh. I'm worried about all this and I can't see any of the kids, yours and mine.'

'Oh, they've got prime seat tickets and they're already inside. Let's join them.'

Inside the hall they showed their tickets to a young official who stared at them with deep suspicion. Simon was surprised to see that the tiered seats were still in place but all the seating at floor level had been removed. On stage a couple of young men were busy assembling loud speaker systems and connecting the electric guitars. These technicians looked surprisingly normal. The hall was rapidly filling

69

with the Swine's fans. Simon saw his little group sitting on a row of tiered seats. He walked up the gangway to them.

'Oh, Dad,' said Lizzie. 'We're allright. You didn't need to watch us.'

'Yes, if you say so, but if there's trouble I'm going to whisk you out of here and back home.'

Cassandra Kellingham spoke. 'Oh, nothing'll happen. It'll be pretty boring I'd say.'

'She's not a Swine fan,' said Lizzie.

'And you are I suppose.'

'Well, they're Ok. I'd rather it'd be the Stones. But I'll give the Swine a fair go and see.'

Hugh spoke. 'Personally I am very interested to hear them. They seem to be very much in tune with today's relevant and aware culture.'

Simon did not know what to think. The three Kellingham kids were immune to adult influence, but he was determined to keep his young free from...from what? No, he was thinking like Lady R-L again.

'All right,' he said. 'But I'd rather you listened from up here and not getting involved with any riot.' He pointed at the level area in front of the stage.

Cassie groaned. 'There won't be any riot.'

'No, Lizzie,' he was firm. 'You will keep a close eye on your brother. He's far too young to be here anyway.'

'No, I'm not,' said Mark. 'I'll be thirteen soon and that's teenage.'

'Yes,' said Simon. 'We will await that with dread.'

Next thing the lights dimmed and then to an uproar of yells and screams the band entered on stage. They looked both weedy and harmless. The three backing players took their instruments and then the lead signer Pete Toilet walked to the microphone. There were more screams and then the alleged concert began. Simon could make little of it. Pete Toilet was a scrawny little fellow with multi-dyed hair. His voice was raucous and Simon was unimpressed by the backing musicians, assuming one could credit them with that title. He remembered the military bandsmen of his regiment had formed a rock group and their standard of playing was a million miles better than these overpaid louts. He forced himself to listen to Toilet singing: *Blast the Palace...* Beside him Hugh was smiling and tapping his shoe to the erratic timing. The children were all straight-faced and nodding in time. They didn't look inclined to riot nor did the mob bopping in front of the stage. An hour passed and Simon looked at his watch.

Thank goodness the supposed time was almost up.

Toilet had carried the microphone on its pole to the front of the stage as he bawled his final chorus.

> *Aw fug*
> *Aw fug fug fug*
> *Awww fug der fug der fug der fugging fug*

Toilet smiled in triumph while the audience screamed. Simon glanced at the faces of the children. They were expressionless but beside him Hugh was smiling. Simon could see the man's lips form the words – *relevant – aware.*

CHAPTER 20

Christmas was a fortnight away. The darkness overwhelmed the village from early evening and the nights were cold. The cottage had a fine fireplace in the front room that burned split logs. Central heating came via a bottled gas system that fired the boiler that in its turn fed the bedroom radiators. Simon had called at a local forestry centre, a business customer and they had given him a very smart Christmas tree. The one thing they were all determined on was that this would be the most memorable family Christmas.

'Dad,' said Lizzie. 'Have you thought of a present for Anna?'

'Your mother and I were discussing that and we thought maybe a little bike for her to ride in summer.'

'If you really want to please her I know what she'd like more than anything.'

'Ok, what?'

'She would love to have a violin. She used to play one when her mum and dad were alive and she said she won prizes for her playing. But then the bloody witch took it and burned it.'

'Liz, watch you language!'

His daughter laughed. 'I remember your language when we were army. You used the f-word a lot.'

'Maybe but we were a lot of macho men. You are a young lady and you should watch your speech.'

She laughed again. 'Yes, don't do as I do. Do as I say.'

'All right, violin? I'll call in the music shop in town, but it'll have to be a cheap and cheerful model; won't be a Strad.'

'Thanks, Dad. We want her to be happy and that'll be great.'

The next day, on the way home from work Simon stopped at the music shop. Violins were plentiful but some obviously of better quality. In the end Simon bought a second-hand instrument that he was assured had once played in a symphony orchestra. Complete with battered case it cost him twenty five pounds. The shop girl offered to have it restrung and tuned and he agreed to collect it in two days time along with some basic music scores. He mused that Anna was such a quiet child but from now on she would hopefully be making some

pleasing sound. The reported power cuts did not seem to have affected Shinkley too badly and he saw that the pub had already put up a chain of coloured lights. Two days on he sneaked the violin indoors and then up into a secluded corner of the attic.

Gladstone Engineering's Christmas party was not an impersonal gathering in the office but a grand affair in the Gladstone family's home. Everyone was invited including wives, partners and children. The Christmas tree in the hallway was so tall it reached to the upper landing on the great staircase. It gleamed with coloured lights and more light chains were everywhere. Simon hoped another power cut would not dampen the joy. At the foot of the tree were piled wrapped presents. Lizzie and Mark already knew many of the invited children from school. While the adults sipped their wine or sank pints of beer the youngsters ran up and down the stairway. It was interesting to sum up the wives of his colleagues. Lorraine, Peter Seldon's other half, was a dumpy middle-aged lady who was already on her fifth glass of red wine. 'Pete's the one driving,' she guffawed. The emotional Sharon was showing off the new boyfriend. He was a smartly dressed farmer's son who looked a mite uncomfortable in this company. She seemed to have completely forgotten Wayne, the lecherous parts salesman, and she was past embarrassing Simon in front of Angie. He had never told his wife about Sharon although Bill's wife had hinted to Angie about her in a jocular fashion. Sharon had never interested Simon, but he felt a twinge of unease. Cyprus; yes, Angie must never know about Melina.

Angie was walking towards him wine glass in hand. 'I've never seen Anna look so happy,' she said. 'She's mixing so well with all the others. I'm so glad that Bill and Sarah invited her as well as our two.'

Simon grinned. 'Wrong. It's our three now. So you won't have to have another.'

Angie threw back her head and gave a rather alcoholic giggle. 'I think I'm a bit old for any more.'

'Nonsense!'

It was Christmas Eve. Simon tiptoed around the bedrooms filling the kids' stockings.

Lizzie obviously had no illusions as to who filled hers but she had insisted on hanging it up anyway. He guessed she was still wide awake as he reached in the cardboard box and pulled out the choc bars, a smart ball-point pen plus a little notebook and finally two oranges. He repeated the progress for the other two younger ones; then

downstairs to pour himself another drink. Tomorrow morning it would be breakfast then church and finally home to unwrap the main presents. Under the guidance of Mrs Gladys Hanbury, the village school head teacher, all the kids had joined with others and gone carol singing. That had meant more choc bars and mince pies. Simon wondered that none of them were sick. He crept silently to the foot of the stairs. A light shone from under the door of Lizzie's bedroom. The alleged Santa Claus had not fooled her. It was now time for Santa himself to get some sleep. Tomorrow would be a long day.

They were home from church. In the kitchen the turkey was maturing in the slow oven. Angie had laden the table with more mince pies and had inserted some lucky coins in the Christmas pudding. The kids had fallen on their presents with wild excitement. These included a succulent bone for Lonny the Labrador. Mark had a new bike with racing drop handlebars, Lizzie had the glamorous party dress that they had promised her and she was preening herself in front of the long mirror. And then to everyone's delight there was Anna with her new violin playing a near perfect rendition of *Hark the Herald Angels Sing*.

'I've suggested we find her a tutor,' said Angie. 'She was excited about that. She tells me she wants to learn to play professionally. You know, classical, not rock.'

Not with the Filthy swine, thank God, thought Simon.

Now both parents glared at Lizzie. She had pulled the strapless top of her dress far too low for their tastes.

'Oi, girl!' Simon shouted. 'Go any further and you'll fall out of that and look a right idiot.'

Lizzie smiled and hitched the dress up a couple of inches. 'If I did that, Gareth would have to pretend to be embarrassed.'

'I hope,' said her mother, 'that you'd be the one embarrassed.'

'No,' said Simon. 'Dress to impress, yes, but not like a tart.'

He turned to Angie. 'God, these teenagers. What are things coming to?'

Angie just laughed. 'You sound really military and definitely Yorkshire. Come on everyone, come and eat Christmas dinner.'

CHAPTER 21

It was now January in the year 1974. Politics that so clouded the life of Shinkley had become obsessive. The Edward Heath government was crumbling in the face of the miners' dispute and the three day week. Power cuts came without warning throughout the day. Simon had imported one of the Gladstone range of generators and had been pleased to be given a healthy discount. He had been forced to move the Rover out of the garage to make room for this machine but it was a huge boon to have it in the crisis. Better still, he had been able to sell a far larger machine to the local council for the Shinkley School.

With this snap election imminent Hugh Kellingham had the demeanour of an excited schoolboy. As Simon had expected Bill Gladstone had refused point blank to run as a candidate for the local Liberals. Christine Kellingham had put her foot down and forbidden Hugh to put his own name forward. His party were now busy interviewing possible runners. Rufus Blanner had been awarded a knighthood in the New Year honours and was definitely not standing. His party had replaced him with Jill Hilldown, the aristocrat's daughter who was also a women's rights campaigner. All Simon could hope for was to keep his head down and wait for the uproar to subside.

Angie was happy in her hospital admin job. Lizzie was progressing well with her school work and thank heavens not being too distracted by the boyfriend, Gareth. Gareth was a burly rugby playing youth and a lot less academic than Lizzie. Mark had settled in well to the village school and had not been worried when other kids mimicked his northern accent. Little Anna had also been well accepted in the school. She could never forget the things she had suffered, but now settled into family life she could move forward. They had found her a music tutor in the town and her violin playing was improving every week. Thank God there was no news of the evil Shartcroft.

'Simon,' said Bill one morning. 'I want us to cash in on this wine making craze. There's several new vineyards being planted in the county and there's a range of specialist vine sprayers coming in from Germany. I've taken one of the franchises.'

Bill showed Simon a number of coloured brochures. 'In May

there's a wine growers conference at Yellwood. I would like you to go and represent us.'

Simon was unsure. 'I know next to nothing about wine growing. There were vineyards near where I was based in Cyprus but they were all red wine and Yellwood only do white.'

Bill grinned. 'Well, now it's your chance to learn the ropes. And you'll have fun. There's a gourmet dinner and some exotic overseas delegations.'

'That sounds better,' said Simon. 'Right, I'll put it in the diary.' At that moment the lights failed. They waited as the powerful generator rolled into action and power was restored.

Simon looked at his employer. 'Bill, Hugh Kellignham wants you to stand for Parliament.'

Bill grinned broadly. 'No thanks, I'm happy with my business. Who really wants to be stuck in that place with all those idiots?'

'You'd be a breath of fresh air.'

'Liberals won't make it here anyway. By-election maybe, but not in the big one. Tory party still rules the roost and anyway Jilly Hilldown is a juicy bird. I quite look forward to taking my problems to her.'

There came another surprise. He arrived home to find Angie had already finished work and had brought Lizzie from school. 'I've got news about that old cow, Shartcroft,' she said.

'Oh, God. I only want to forget her.'

'Well, you can for a bit longer. Chris told me Shartcroft has had her remission cancelled. Seems she was carrying on a lesbian relationship with a prison guard. And she's assaulted and seriously injured another prisoner. But she's American by nationality and it's likely she'll be deported on release. Or we can hope.'

'Best thing, but hell she must have needed a man to get herself conceived...' Simon was interrupted as once again the lights failed. A short pause and he smiled as his beloved generator fired up and brought new light with it.

Now the General Election campaign was in full swing. Simon wanted nothing to do with it and was not happy to discover that Lizzie was going out with Cassandra Kellingham canvassing for the Liberals. Fortunately they went as a team covering an area and there were several responsible adults with them. With extreme reluctance he agreed to go to the debate in Shinkley village hall. Here all three main party candidates would argue their causes with the tenacity of those

who believed the world to be flat. Thank goodness the BPP man was not invited and a local police constable would prevent him or any other extremists gate-crashing the meeting. His army experience had made Simon a good judge of character. If he had to go to this event he would sum up these candidates and then vote for the least obnoxious.

It was a wet mid-February evening and at least the hall was warm. The actual polling day was still a week away. The hall was not as crowded as it had been for the Common Market debate but at least two thirds of the seats were taken. Clearly several blocks of voters were only there to cheer for their own side. These people Simon could ignore.

The same local doctor as last time had been coerced to take the chair. The participants were already seated and were invited one at a time to state their case. The Labour man was a diminutive figure who orated in a comedian's Lancashire accent. He had a great deal to say about "public ownership" and something he called "the Tread Yonion movement". Then there was Hugh Kellingham's Liberal. The man was a moderately eloquent local lawyer. He seemed a likeable fellow but had very little of substance to say.

Lastly called to speak was the runaway favourite to win, the Conservative Jill Hilldown. He had to admit that the woman was rather glamorous to be an MP but she spoke in those icy cut-glass tones that marked her out as an aristocrat. And like the other two she had very little to say except that in her opinion the Tories were destined to rule and Labour to mess things up. Simon yawned.

Next the chair called for questions. There was a long period of silence and then he saw Stefanie from the new sisterhood stand up. 'Mrs Hilldown, your father is an earl and you are his eldest child. Yet when sadly he passes on you won't have his privileged title. It will pass to Nigel your younger brother. Isn't this the most unfair discrimination against women?'

Jill Hilldown threw back her head and laughed. 'When my brother Nigel inherits he will be bound for the stuffy upper house. I feel liberated in that I can be a member of the House of Commons that takes the real decisions. I, like you, am a campaigner for women and there I will have my say and my influence.' The speech attracted warm applause even from among the ranks of her opponents.

Simon was still undecided when the meeting ended. He was one of millions who had to decide the nation's future at a critical moment. He still didn't like politicians but he didn't think spinning a coin would be a good idea. Go home and sleep on it was all he could do.

After much blatant mental bullying from Lizzie and some loyalty to his Kellingham friends Simon put his cross against the Liberal. He was unsure about this and didn't enquire about Angie's choice.

The election result was predictable. Jill Hilldown won locally with a slightly reduced majority with Hugh's Liberals second and the Labour man just saving his deposit. The BPP man trailed way behind with just one hundred and forty votes. Nationally the country faced its first experience of a hung parliament. After several days of argument Labour, the largest party, took over Government under Prime Minister Harold Wilson. Perhaps life could now return to normal.

CHAPTER 22

Simon and Angie had almost fully adapted to life in these strange Southern parts. Angie was fully involved with the local WI and both were doing work for the British Legion. Simon had been both surprised and pleased to find how many retired ex-servicemen lived in the area and surroundings. Many of these were involved in agriculture and related industries and this had helped him in his day-to-day business. Work on the farms had been flat out these last three months as the arable men drilled in spring sown crops and fertilised and sprayed the autumn sown ones.

It was Sunday afternoon and now spring was here and noticeably earlier than in Yorkshire; daffodils bloomed and shrubs coloured with flowers while already buds were breaking into green leaves. Simon grinned and checked himself. All these thoughts were far too lyrical for a true born Yorkshire man. But hell, life here in the South was good. He was busy giving himself a crash course in wine making. The conference at Yellwood Vineyards was in May and Bill had high hopes of doing good business there.

Today it was warm enough to sit in the garden and later he would need to mow the lawn. For the first time this year all the house windows were open and he could hear Anna's violin playing Mendelssohn. Her music had really changed Anna's life, that of course and best of all finding a happy settled home. Suddenly the violin missed a beat and then slurred into a discord. 'Hi, Lonny,' Anna shouted. 'Get down. You can have your walk in a minute.'

The sun was still shining as Simon arrived at Yellwood. Just south of the line of the Downs this was a warm spot ideal for the thirty-five acre vineyard. This was the dream of the multi-millionaire owner and it was impressive. The owner had lashed out over two hundred thousand pounds alone on a beautiful Cotswold Stone building packed full of presses and stainless steel vats imported from the continent. Simon was in the native British contingent being shown the sights. Ahead of them was a mixed European group made up of wine experts from Spain, France, Germany and Greece. This evening all would sit down to a gourmet dinner with wine. When they met the vineyard

manager Simon had brochures for the brand new fan-assisted vine sprayer. These sprays were to tackle the fungal infections that could destroy a whole crop. He understood that this vineyard was presently employing a force of underpaid immigrants to spray the vines by hand. What future there was for wine production in England was still uncertain but these people were going for it with professionalism that was impressive.

Dusk was approaching when all present were ushered into a new entertainment centre and Simon caught the aroma of dinner from the adjacent kitchen. He accepted one glass of wine. Angie had lectured him that morning on drink driving and the penalties for those caught. The room was filling with a united-nations gathering. Simon caught the jabber of foreign languages not a word of which he knew. Suddenly he was aware of someone staring at him from across the room. He turned and received a shock that nearly floored him. A beautiful dark-haired girl was looking at him, no not looking; she was smiling in recognition. My God, Melina. In a dreamlike state he walked across to her.

She smiled at him all the way as he walked across the room. Oh, she was so beautiful. Her long dark hair, full lips and little elfin nose and her lovely slim body. He couldn't think properly so great was the shock.

'Hello,' she said. 'Is it you, is it Simon, Captain Rosy?'

He recalled her good spoken English and again her total inability to pronounce his family name. 'Hello, Melina, yes it's me. But how did you get here?'

'I am working in the wine. I know we come to England but this is a surprise.'

Memories were streaming back. He recalled the tensions of patrolling in Cyprus; then returning to base and his meeting, by chance with this lovely girl. He knew their friendship had put her in danger from Eoka but she had not worried. Diffident at first she had relaxed in his company until that lovely warm July night when they had stripped and both swum naked in the warm Mediterranean. Still wet they had lain on their towels in the moonlit shadow of a rock and made love. Following this he had been careless and there had been talk in the regiment. Colonel Cohen had warned him the girl might be a covert agent after military secrets. But instinctively Simon knew that this was not so. Melina's love was real. She asked no questions about his soldiering but both knew their attraction was doomed. She had severe Greek Orthodox parents and she knew that back home he was

married. Now they were meeting again in the strangest of surround-ings and that Angie must never know.

'So you are in the wine business,' he said.

'Oh yes, and you must know that I work here in England for six months.' She tilted her head and smiled. 'Can we still be friends?'

'You look a bit light-headed,' said Angie. 'What did you drink and was it a good party?'

Angie was as always far too perceptive.

'It was interesting and they certainly served a good dinner.' Yes, he had sat down to dinner but some places away from Melina. It had been a gourmet spread and he had relished it. He suddenly felt like a small boy who had been caught scrumping apples. Following the meal he'd spoken to Melina again. 'We are both married now,' she had said. 'But I hope we can be friends.'

He was torn in two. Was it good news that the girl was married? Well yes, it put them on the same level. But could they really meet and be platonic friends?

'You still look a bit dreamy,' said his wife. 'How did your sales trip go?'

He was jerked back into the real world. 'Bill'll be pleased. I sold two round fan sprayers. We should have them for the vineyard in a week.'

It was nearly eleven o'clock. He tiptoed upstairs and peeped in the children's rooms. All three had been sleeping peacefully. No, he knew where his duty and his heart lay. He had treasure in this house and family and he would do nothing to spoil that.

CHAPTER 23

We haven't passed the deadline for council nominations,' said Hugh. 'Parish council, Simon – how about it?'

'If I do, it won't be for a political party.'

'No, only the really big towns and villages have a party candidates list. You would be standing as yourself.'

Angie joined the fray. 'Hugh, I think he should. He's already contributed to life by demolishing that Shartcroft witch. Everyone knows about that and us taking in Anna.'

'That's true,' said Hugh. 'I can tell you they all like you here.'

'All right, I'll give it a go.'

For the rest of that day he worried. Was he overreaching himself? He had resolved to have nothing to do with politics but surely even a village council was politics. Hardly inspiring either. Keep the drains clean, keep the street lights burning. Block any speculative building development. None of this was epoch shaping.

All three children were home from school and Lizzie had brought Cassandra with her plus a heavy box-like object. 'It's a tape recorder,' said Lizzie. 'We've got tapes of the Stones and the Beatles and Barry White and the Three Degrees and lots more.'

Simon grunted. 'What about the Filthy Swine?'

Lizzie grimaced. 'No thanks, they didn't do much for us that time.'

He looked at Anna, 'That's rock – not your sort of music surely?'

'Why not, a lot of it I like.'

'All right; just keep the volume down please.'

He walked downstairs and a minute later there came the warbling tones of David Essex singing: *Gonna make you a star.*

He sat down in the kitchen with a cup of tea.

Angie glanced at him. 'You sounded ever so grumpy talking to the kids.'

'I suppose it's advancing years. I don't really mind that music.' He frowned. 'Why won't Anna still not wear shoes?'

'Why should she? The summer's here it's warm and barefoot is much healthier.'

'I suppose so. I just hope she keeps away from thorn bushes and snakes.'

Angie laughed and waved her own shoeless foot in his face.

'That's disgusting,' he snorted.

During the Easter holidays all three children had their first taste of sailing. Simon had paid for them to take an official course at a sailing school on nearby Hayling Island. This had been in very heavy and safe instructional boats and the kids had loved it. Now they had the summer in front of them and their own little Cadet dinghy based at the nearby yacht club. The Kellinghams: Cassie, Max and Tammie had an identical boat and so did Bill Gladstone's young ones. The three families looked forward to some competition on the water as well as more trips in Bill's big yacht. They learned that Lizzie's Gareth also sailed a similar Mirror Dinghy. Simon still had doubts but it seemed that Gareth was harmless and was more interested in his sports than he was in Lizzie. They were a handsome pair. Lizzie had the same fair hair and similar features to her mother but now at fifteen she was definitely a beauty. He, of course was prejudiced but others remarked on this too. Mark was now playing for the village school's cricket team. He could bowl a bit and was the team's top scorer. Simon smiled. That was good and very Yorkshire. Anna was already a fine violinist and was due to play at the school's end of term concert. Simon still felt occasional nostalgia for the army, but no. This was the life for him, his wife and family and Shinkley for all its quirks was the right place for them.

The telephone rang at seven am. Who on earth? Simon slid out of bed and pulled on his dressing gown. It was cold and the central heating has not fired up yet. Angie lay sleeping – nothing would wake her until she was ready to awake. He stumbled downstairs and picked up the phone in his tiny office room. 'Hello, Simon,' it was Hugh speaking.

'Hello, Hugh and it's bloody early.'

'I know, sorry about that but did you hear those police sirens a while back.'

Simon frowned. 'It's funny you should say that but I did sort of hear something. Do you know what it's about?'

'Sorry, no, but there were three police cars and they all shot up Rufus Blanner's driveway.'

Simon was unimpressed. 'I suppose some thief has broken in and stolen a flower vase. He's the ex-MP with a knighthood so I suppose that constitutes an emergency.'

Simon asked Hugh to keep him in touch and then staggered back to bed. In an hour's time he would have to get up for real and run Lizzie to her school.

Later that day Television Southern News reported that police had been called to Shinkley Manor after shots had been fired. No one it seemed had been hurt and the police would issue a statement when they were ready. Simon shrugged his shoulders and from Gladstone's office he arranged for an upstairs extension phone to be fitted in the bedroom. He did not know then that this would be a decision that would come back to haunt him. On the Thursday of that week polling took place for the district and parish councils. Simon's name had gone forward for the parish and Hugh Kellingham's for the District Council. Simon had not actively campaigned. It was for the people to decide. Either they liked this North-country foreigner or they did not. Angie and he attended the counting of votes in the village hall. The procedure took a couple of hours with a satisfactorily high turnout. Hugh took the district council seat with an eighty vote majority. Then came the parish results. Simon had approached this moment with genuine indifference. And incredibly, top of the poll was one Simon Robsby with three hundred and thirty-two votes. It took his a good twenty minutes to comprehend.

Outside the hall he saw Kevin the local village copper. 'What happened the other day up at the Manor?' he asked. 'Nobody seems to know a thing, not even the local rag.'

Kevin grinned. 'Seems there was a big falling out among the harem. I dunno' how that old geezer does it. Anyway one of them girls took the boss's shot gun and loosed off at her rival.'

Simon also did not know what it was that drew these girls to the lecherous old Blabbermouth. He supposed it was love of money more than sexual attraction. 'Anyone hurt?'

'No, it was all drama. She fired up in the air and then chased the other girl around the gardens. Then the old man sent for us. I'm telling you this in confidence mind. Blabbermouth doesn't want any charges made.'

Well, he was a parish councillor now. Shinkley was weird but he must do his best for it weird or not. He did not know that Nemesis was about to strike.

CHAPTER 24

It was a warm Sunday morning when Simon sat in his office cubby hole and the phone rang. Not business today, he hoped.

'Simon, Simon Rosy. Is that you?'

Simon stiffened both physically and mentally. He knew that voice: Melina.

'Look, you shouldn't ring me here and anyway where are you?'

'Oh, Simon please you not to be angry. I am staying in a nice hotel in Mid Hurst and I would like to talk to you.' The voice was soft and almost hypnotic.

'What do you want with me?'

'I only want to talk with you. I need no funny business. Please come eat a meal at this good place.'

He sighed. 'All right, but it mustn't be a habit. As you know now I'm no longer in the army and I'm living a happy life with my family.'

'Oh, Simon, me too. I am working here and I just want to talk. No funny business – we talk old times.'

'How do you know where I live – this phone number.'

'I am working for Mercurio. We sell you British the best wine techniques. I rang the office of Mister Gladstone and they gave me your number.'

He took a deep breath. 'Look Melina, I can't see you today but I could tell my wife that I've an evening call out tomorrow.' He put the phone down his head now in the metaphorical whorl. Thank God, Angie was down the road with the Kellinghams and the children were all safe in the bedrooms upstairs. With luck, he could get away with this secret tryst.

Simon spent an anxious day unable to really concentrate on work. He only hoped nobody in the office noticed. What the hell was he thinking of in meeting this girl who was an embarrassment from his past. She had sounded so plaintive and it could do no harm to meet her on neutral ground as it were. He reached the hotel on the outskirts of Midhurst at seven thirty and parked his car. What should he do now? Well, he and Melina had an illicit past relationship but that was many years ago and, yes, it would be good to see her again. And there she

was sitting on a sofa in the corner of the main lounge.

Melina was on her feet and ran across to him. She reached up and gave a soft kiss on his cheek. She was beautiful with her styled dark hair. She wore a smart dark blue business suit with short skirt and strappy high-heels.

'Oh, Simon. Such a shock I had when I see you that time.'

'Bit of a shock for me too.'

'You are still handsome man – still like the soldier.'

'Steady on, Melina. I'm not a soldier anymore and I have a wife and family.'

'Do they know I see you today?'

'No they do not. Angela, my wife doesn't know you ever existed.'

'I too have a man I marry, but I told him about you.'

'Did he mind?'

'No.'

Simon sighed. He couldn't make head no tail of this girl. She had aged very little since he'd known her before. 'How about family? Have you any children?'

'No, I travel the world for business – so no time.'

'That's sad.'

They took their places in the dining room and the waiter served a tasty fish soup. For most of the meal they ate in silence although Simon was conscious of Melina looking at him covertly throughout. Gradually he relaxed as they talked of times in Cyprus. He told her of his new life and his family. He was surprised to learn that she had been in England at the time of the Shartcroft trial but had not known that his family were involved.

'That woman was evil,' she sighed. 'She fights for women but I live in world of men and I earn money – do Ok.'

Simon knew he was falling for her as he admired her beauty and her slim figure and long legs. But she did not invite him upstairs and he hoped he would have enough resolve to decline the temptation had it been dangled in front of him. They talked on about life and work and the past and future. Then he said goodnight and this time outside in the dark she kissed full on the mouth with tongue and Mediterranean passion. 'Simon, I never forget you.' She stood there a solitary figure as he drove into the street and started the twenty mile journey home.

It was a quarter past eleven when he reached home. He was surprised that all the house lights were still burning. He walked inside and there

was Angie staring at him in a less than welcoming look. 'You didn't stay the night then,' she said. For a second a very faint smile flickered across her face.

'Well no.'

'That at least is something, I suppose.' Again that odd smile. 'Tell me, how is Melina?'

Now he felt real shock and horror. He knew his mouth was dropping open. 'How on earth?'

Angie smacked the flat of her hand on the table. And now he saw the kid's tape recorder. Angie pressed the start button and he heard his voice and Melina's. It was a recording of his phone conversation with her. 'How on earth?'

'Lizzie and Cassie were having a laugh and they thought they'd try and record a message on that new extension. What they heard they didn't like much and they brought it to me this morning.'

Simon had been caught, bang to rights as they said in films. 'I'm sorry but the girl is by way of being a work colleague she represents Mercurio the wine press makers...'

'No, bullshit!! She's your fancy girl that you were knocking off in Cyprus.'

His mouth dropped open again. His humiliation was complete. 'How did you know? You've never said.'

'Everyone knew. Esme Cohen told me at the Regimental dinner. She was amused but she thought I should know. Her husband wasn't much better but she said his whore was ugly and yours was rather pretty,'

'Why haven't you said anything before?'

Now she laughed but there was no humour in it. 'We army wives know what soldiers are like and what they get up to overseas. Less said the better. In the war my dad fought in Italy. Mum knew he was knocking off Italian maidens so she had her own fling with a Polish officer. I can just remember him. He was nice and gave me chocolate when it was hard to get.'

He felt the tears well up and then run down his face. 'Oh I am sorry, but Angie I've always loved you. There'll never be anyone else. Please, what are you going to do?'

'Do, I'm not doing anything. I'd rather like to meet this Melina. From what Esme says she was quite a dish.'

However undignified he was now on his knees before her. 'Oh please, don't leave. I love you. That girl was nothing. It's only you I've ever loved.'

87

She gave him a less than playful slap around his head. 'Get up and stop that grovelling. I've kept a close eye on you since you came home and I can't fault you. Since you didn't stay with the girl tonight, I think you're cured of her. So, we go forward as if it hadn't happened but I will still be watching, so remember!'

'What do the children know about all this?

'I told them it was only a call from a friend who is also a business associate and made them promise never to do it again.'

'Thank you, my love.'

They went upstairs to bed and then to almost to his surprise they made love as passionately as they once had long ago.

CHAPTER 25

1975

A whole year and a half had now passed since the family's arrival in Shinkley. Simon to his surprise was enjoying his role on the parish council. He had been able to help local people with council-related problems and those outside his remit he could pass on to Hugh Kellingham. A further general election had taken place later in 1974. Jill Hilldown had been returned with an increased majority despite the misogynist element in her own local party.

Bill Gladstone had praised Simon and given him a substantial salary increase even though that meant paying more in tax. Much more important was the family. They were in the final stages of a formal adoption of Anna. They had spoken to her about this several times and she made it clear this was the one thing she craved. In a few week's time she would be Anna Robsby. Anna had been auditioned and accepted and was now playing in the county youth orchestra. Her new brother and sister were progressing well at their schools and Lizzie was due to take GCE O level in July. They had spent happy hours sailing their little dinghy on the harbour sometimes racing against the Kellingham and Gladstone children but no longer against the boy Gareth with whom Lizzie had fallen out over a rival girl.

Simon had never felt closer to his wife. He so admired her self-confidence when she sought out Melina just before the Cypriot girl returned to her home country. They had all met in a café in the town and though Simon had been apprehensive from the start he had marvelled as the two girls seemed to hit it off, as his Lizzie might say. Cyprus was now peaceful and they had discussed a holiday there. Best news of all was that Shartcroft had returned to America. Not deported but by her own choice. They had heard that she was now in a feminist group in New York.

The Shinkley Sisterhood had been transformed by Tessa and Stefanie who were their own friends. Far from being against men both girls had male partners. Very loyal partners they proved. They were expected to do house cleaning and shopping for the commune. The BPP had continued to spread hate. Their campaign against Bill

Gladstone seemed to have had no effect with his farming customers.

He could hear Angie's voice. It was raised in semi-anger. 'No, Lizzie. It's wrong and she will live to regret it. What's more you will live to regret if you're ever so stupid.'

Lizzie hurtled downstairs rather dangerously and fled out of the house. 'What's going on?' he called.

Angie came downstairs and her expression was grim. 'Cassandra's been boasting at school. Claims she's had sex with her boyfriend.'

'Is it true? You know kids do boast.'

'Not sure, but her parents have this free and easy ethos. The girl's in her last year before university and she claims her parents have put her on the pill.'

'Well, that's better than getting up the duff and blowing her career and future.'

'Simon. Listen to me. That's not the point. I'm not doing that for Lizzie – no way. She's got to resist. Boys are lecherous, girls are vulnerable.'

'Not all boys surely.'

'Oh, yes. What were you like in your Sandhurst days, soldier?'

'We were worked twenty-four seven and we were far too exhausted to try anything. They didn't have girls there in my time either.'

'What about later. When you joined the regiment?'

He laughed, probably not very convincingly. 'I was a very good boy.'

'Until you met Melina? I bet she wasn't the only one. You knew how to please a girl when we first married. Someone showed you how.'

'Well, you lapped it up – never complained.'

Now she grinned. 'Oh, yes. We enjoyed ourselves all night. But I have a duty to Lizzie and I'll keep her safe.' She stalked into the front room muttering. 'Bloody men.'

'You sound like the Sisterhood,' he called.

Simon stood up and walked into the garden. He was feeling stiff in limb nowadays. He was unfit. Maybe he should take up cross-country running again. He had put on weight this last year having long ago left behind route marches and assault courses. He could hear the sound of police sirens and moments later two police cars and an ambulance raced past up the road out of the village. He shrugged, well nothing to do with Rufus Blanner this time. He assumed a road accident. Half and hour later the ambulance returned at speed, lights flashing. Then the two police cars came past. Presumably both parties were on their

way to town: the ambulance to accident and emergency and the police to their home base. Simon walked back indoors. It was time for his Sunday morning whisky.

The news filtered around Shinkley that evening. Simon and Angie could not really believe it. The obnoxious Wally Fircomb had been seriously injured in a road accident. Well maybe serve him right. Then they took in the unbelievable gossip that in Simon's opinion couldn't be true. Fircomb had been run off the road into a tree. It was an intended assault and not by an enemy of the BBP but by a Landrover driven by one of his own thugs. It was reported that Fircomb had had a Damascus road revelation. He had repudiated Hitler and racism and sought God. That couldn't be true. It was mad.

On Monday Simon learned the astonishing truth. He visited a farm that was the work place of the local monastery. Simon arranged the delivery of a new bale elevator and completed the details with the lay manager.

'You live in Shinkley?' the man asked.

'Yes.'

'You've heard about Fircomb?'

'Well, yes, but I don't know what to believe.'

'It's true. He's been talking to Father Edmund in the Cathedral for a couple of months. Seems he's rejected all the Nazi stuff and found Jesus.'

Simon was baffled. Found Jesus who was a Jew! This was some turn around by any standards. 'Last we've heard is that Fircomb is in hospital. Seems one of his thugs tried to kill him.'

'Will that be the end of the BPP?'

'Well,' said Simon, 'We can live in hope.'

The newspapers and Television were full of the political situation. Edward Heath seemed doomed as his party rejected him and replaced him with Margaret Thatcher. 'Jill Hilldown was full of it,' said Hugh Kellingham, 'but I doubt that'll last long. Thatcher's no feminist. She's all male in her attitude.' Simon still really didn't care.

The local press was full of the Fircomb accident, not any talk of religious conversion but it seemed one of the BPP thugs had been charged with assault and dangerous driving. Fircomb was in the local hospital and was said to be recovering from a back injury. All that was known was that Fircomb had resigned the leadership of the BPP. The press had hinted at internal divisions. Simon had made a road diversion and sneaked past the BPP headquarters. The burly guards

with their baseball bats were missing. The place looked deserted. He wondered if some long overdue sanity was returning to Shinkley.

The day had finally arrived. Anna was a full member of the Robsby family. She had long merged into their life as a much more self-confident and mischievous little girl. Anna could not entirely escape her past. She was prone to occasional depression and sometimes nightmares. She was devoted to her new home and really grateful for the life that had been given her. Simon and Angie took it in turns to drive her to the rehearsals of the county youth orchestra. The lady conductor had taken Angie aside and assured her that Anna had a great future in music. She must keep up her practice and then she was certain of a career in adulthood. Well adulthood was a long way off. Today Anna was going with family and a huge contingent of friends for a christening ceremony in the chapel. Before embarking on this they had talked to Anna and she had assured them she enjoyed going to the chapel and singing hymns and of course she had played a solo violin recital in there at Easter attended by so many from the village..

The skeleton at the feast was of course the appalling Shartcroft. Dan Lederman's wife at the local paper had discovered that Shartcroft was part of feminist academy in Brooklyn. These American women had apparently devised semi-religious ceremonies reciting a bowdlerised Lord's or rather Lady's prayer beginning: *Our mother who art always on earth* and ending *deliver us from men – for ever and ever – awomen.* How did New York's largely male culture react to this? They would, he guessed mostly ignore it. Live and let live was that city's ethos.

They drove Anna to the chapel. She was attired in a new white dress and of course she had been prevailed upon to wear a pair of neat white shoes. Mark and Lizzie were smartly dressed while their parents had bought themselves new suits for the occasion. All their friends had turned out for the ceremony and the party later. Even the agnostic Kellinghams were there. Their children were for once modestly dressed and even Hugh had been prevailed upon to wear a tie. Jill Hilldown the local MP had been invited and to everyone's surprise she was there. Not so welcome was a TV crew and three news reporters. It seemed Shartcroft and Shinkley were not forgotten.

They greeted Hugh and Christine. Hugh looked puzzled. 'Anna looks smart today but I thought people were baptised by totally dunking them in water.'

Bill Gladstone chuckled. 'No, that's a lot called Baptists. I imagine

these people just sprinkle a bit of holy wet stuff. I don't know. I'm a Catholic but I guess that's what this lot do as well.'

'Mr Gladstone, you are spot on,' said Mrs Hobbs, the minister's wife.

'That's a relief,' said Hugh. 'We won't get splashed then.'

'Now, Hugh,' said Chris his wife. 'We all said we would be respectful, did we not?'

Simon in his turn laughed. 'It's all this relevant and awareness.'

The religious ceremony over, they all retired to the small annexe of the village hall. Angie with Chris and several other village ladies had prepared a glorious spread of party food. Anna, Lizzie and Mark, with the Kellingham and Gladstone kids plus a contingent of friends fell on this, especially the chocolate cakes. The adults sipped wine, drank tea and chewed on the ham sandwiches. Kevin the village copper stood outside the door to frighten off the press.

Mr Hobbs, the minister shook hands with Simon and Angie. He was grinning. 'Our Mr Kellingham over there says he's an unbeliever. I have a lovely dream that on the day he passes on he'll hear a clap of thunder and a then see blinding light. Then a voice roars: "Hello Hugh, you don't believe in me, well, take a good look".'

Anna had really come alive, more than at any time since she had joined the family. She chattered to everyone, was allowed a tiny sip of wine that only made her grimace and then she was handed her violin and played her own selection of Beatles melodies. The Kellinghams seemed to get on famously with Jill Hilldown. Simon's cynicism reckoned politicians might hurl insults at each other and the other's parties but they were all the same under the skin. Stefanie and Tess from the new sisterhood were there and with them came their male partners. Contrary to everything he'd heard Simon found these two, Mike and Joe, to be self-assured and amusing company. With the food gone and the talk exhausted Simon and Angie gathered up the whole united family and all drove happily home.

CHAPTER 26

All hope that the BBP might have died with the defection of its leader were stilled. A new leader had moved into the Shinkley headquarters and was breeding even more hate. For Simon this had reached a head when a Gladstone delivery lorry was firebombed at a village in East Sussex. It was a remote site where the driver had left his charge to ask directions. He returned to find his lorry on fire. Bravely the man had unlashed the tractor on the rear of the lorry and driven it to ground level. This was not the only incident and now the police felt able to raid the BPP house and arrest the new leader. They were unable to prove a definite connection to the vandalism although forensics found an empty drum of petrol in a diesel powered van. In the end the BPP man was released threatening more hate.

'The cops have been supportive,' said Bill. 'They patrol past our house at night. Our local Bobbies are decent. Not like the Met. There's covert BPP support among some of the older police up there. Here the Lederman's have had to have their telephone moved ex-directory and the old man has had the synagogue alarm system linked direct to the central police station. '

Simon wasn't satisfied. 'It's all wrong – you or they shouldn't have to put up with this.'

'I know but the support we've had locally is amazing. These Nazi fanatics are damaging themselves with the people around here.'

At home there had been a nervous few days for Lizzie as she waited for her O level results. Then the great day when she learned she had passed with distinction in maths and also in English, physics and biology. Simon who in his day had just scraped by with the old School Certificate wondered where all this genius had sprung from. Mark would be joining his sister in the senior school in the autumn while Anna still had one more year with the Shinkley school. Cassie Kellingham was off to university in Bristol. Cassie's enthusiasm for the campaigning CND had worried Simon and Angie. So far they had restrained Lizzie from going along with all this. Not that Simon was a fan of nuclear warfare. If everything was shrivelled in flame in the first hour of war there wouldn't be much call for traditional soldiering.

Cassie still had a lot to learn about the real world. From everything that Brigadier Cohen had told him, the Soviets held their Eastern European empire by bluff, plus nuclear threat and not much else.

The news that Simon had concealed from his family could no longer be hidden. 'Angie, I've ten days summer holiday coming up in two weeks. It'll still be school holidays then. How say we take the kids away to somewhere warm.'

Angie looked pleased. 'I wondered if Bill had forgotten you'd been working for him for a whole year.'

'How about a trip down to the Med. You know Spain or Portugal, Corsica maybe.'

Angie had her most malicious expression. 'Wait a minute I've got an idea but it's written down and in my desk drawer.' Angie rummaged there for a moment and then found a small notebook. 'Now, how about Amathus Bay.'

'That's in Cyprus, but it's some way from where we were based and I believe it's quiet. You know, not so many drunks and rowdy night spots.'

Angie was grinning now. 'When we met your little Melina she told me her relations run a very nice little hotel in that place and if we wanted to holiday there she would get us a discount.'

Simon was stunned. Would he ever understand this amazing girl? 'I thought that would be the last place you wanted to go.'

'Not so. I think and hope you are cured from that lady and she was lyrical about this Amathus Bay place. A few weeks later she sent me a brochure.' She laughed. 'I made sure you never saw it.'

Simon considered this seriously. Yes, he was cured of Melina or at least he had no desire to bed her. And he loved Cyprus despite the dangers of his anti-terrorist patrols. But that was old history now. Yes, why not: warm seas sunny beaches, nice suntans.

'Look, no way am I contacting Melina, but if you really fancy the idea. I'll let you make the waves as it were.'

Angie smiled and clapped her hands. 'Amathus Bay here we come.'

The heat was the shock as they disembarked at Larnaca. Angie removed the blindfold from Anna's face. The poor little girl had been frightened at the idea of an air flight. They could all understand that. Anna had lost both her parents in a single air disaster. She had snuggled against Angie for the whole flight duration and had hardly

moved. UK residents did not require visas and they passed through customs with no questions. Simon could recall just enough Greek to collect and pay for their ancient Renault hire car. His Yorkshire accent did not help and the little girl in the garage almost had hysterics. Then of course she had replied in fluent English. With a somewhat chastened Simon behind the wheel they had driven off along the coast road for their holiday destination.

Angie had rung ahead from the airport and she had been answered by, who else, but Melina. This she concealed from her husband. They arrived at the resort and after a few wrong turns and a stop to ask direction they reached the little whitewashed guest house a stone's throw from a lovely smooth beach. And who was it waiting with a wide smile – Melina. Lizzie, nudged her mother and hissed an all too audible stage whisper. 'Is that Dad's fancy girl?'

Simon wished that he could shrink to invisibility. Angie gave the daughter a mild clip around the ear. 'I told you, no mention!'

Simon, in spite of the searing heat felt cold. 'How in hell...?'

'Well, I've got ears haven't I.' Lizzie sounded defiant.

'Yes,' said her mother. 'And your ears have been flapping while your parents talked in confidence.'

Melina welcomed them each in turn with no special greeting for Simon. 'Come indoors.'

They were pleased to find the guest house had air conditioning and was deliciously cool after the heat of the outside. Here they met Melina's cousins, two bubbly middle-aged ladies called: Andrea and Kari. Both wore full length gowns of light material and were clearly not sun worshippers. Next they were shown their rooms. Lizzie and Anna shared while Mark had a little cubby hole of his own and Simon and Angie a full-sized room with a fine double bed. They unpacked and went down to the outside terrace where the adults sipped a pleasant mature red wine and the youngsters drank orange juice with ice. The sun was setting to Westward and they could see the last light reflected on the white sands. 'This really is special,' said Angie.

'I know,' he said. 'Ten days of heaven and then back to Shinkley: parish council and grumbling farmers.'

'It feels so peaceful,' said Angie. 'But isn't this still a troubled land?'

'Oh, yes. We left in 1960 but they allowed us to keep our military bases. The north is Turkish Cypriot and there's always been tension between the two before the mainland Turks moved in and took over the north.. The Greeks don't like it but there's little that they can do.

Anyway, it won't affect us staying here.'

Angie gazed around. 'Where's Melina gone?'

'Oh, don't worry. I saw her drive off in the direction of Limassol. That's where she and her husband are living.'

She leaned across and kissed him. 'Not three of us in a bed then.'

Simon laughed. 'Lovely thought but I haven't the energy.'

The next morning they awoke to dazzling sunshine. They all showered and dressed in their beachwear. The breakfast was true Mediterranean seafood, a real contrast to back home and all voted it delicious. The hotel supplied them with a packed lunch and an ice box with more wine and soft drink. Angie supervised in turn the covering of her husband and the children with sun screen and then they made their way the few steps to the beach. They all wore dressing gowns covering swim suits. Then Lizzie slid off hers and revealed... 'What the hell is that?' Simon roared. The girl was wearing a bikini, yes, but this one consisted of thin string holding together four tiny cloth triangles.

Lizzie turned and smiled at them. Her look was almost demure. 'It's French,' she said. 'Cassie Kellingham gave it to me when she heard we were coming here. Don't you like it?'

'Girl, one sneeze and the whole thing'll fall apart.'

Simon gasped again as his wife revealed a bikini not a lot more modest. 'Oh come on, love,' she said. Then she knelt down and whispered. 'Melina told me you two frolicked around starkers.'

That was true of course. At least Anna wore a pretty little blue swimsuit and Mark was attired in modest shorts very similar to those he wore himself.

CHAPTER 27

Return to England was not so depressing. They arrived at Gatwick in the early hours and recovered the garaged Rover. Yes, it had been a holiday in paradise but it was so good to be home. 'I'll take the films to be developed tomorrow,' said Simon.

'Holiday snaps,' laughed Angie. 'Now I can bore all our friends.'

'No, they'll be so jealous,' said Lizzie. 'They'll see me in my bikini.'

'All those glamour model poses,' said her mother. 'More likely they'll fall about laughing.'

They all had memories. The sunshine, the swimming and building amazing sun tans. Sailing in a catamaran, and then ashore eating wonderful meals. Then they had met Melina and her husband Costas, a business man and director of Mercurio the firm his wife travelled for. Most of Simon's embarrassment had gone. They were grateful to Melina for this holiday even if she was almost, but not yet a true family friend. Now he was turning the car into their short driveway. They were home.

They had hardly stepped indoors when the phone rang. Simon answered and heard the voice of Peter Seldon. 'Simon, you're home thank God.'

Simon was alert. The usually ebullient Peter sounded grim. 'Your father-in-law's been trying to find you. Seems your ma-in-law's poorly.'

'You'd better talk to Angie.' He gestured to her and then handed over the phone.

She listened and grimaced. 'How bad is it?'

'All right, I'll arrange to come north. I need to be there with her.'

She replaced the phone and pulled a wan face. 'Mum's had a mild stroke but they don't think it's life-threatening. She's in a hospital in Bradford and I must see her. She's been asking for me.'

Simon was shocked. Mary Leacrum, Angie's mother, was sixty but she was tough. Nobody had expected this. Mary was an outdoor girl a farm livestock handler. 'You'd better go tomorrow,' he said. 'Can I drive you?'

'That's nice of you to offer, but you can't. There's three children

needing looking after. You've got to be here.'

'I don't think you ought to do the drive in the Anglia. Can you take the train? You'll have to cross London to Kings Cross...'

'Oh, stop fussing! I've done the trip to London before several times when I was not much more than Lizzie's age. I'll meet dad in Bradford and he'll drive me home. Anyway, come next school holidays I've said we'll all go north together and then you can drive us. That'll be nearer to Christmas and they haven't met Anna yet.'

Simon knew that it was traditional for a man to be irritated by a mother-in-law; but not in this case. He had always liked Mary and had been secretly amused to hear about the lady's wartime love life. It all fitted with a sparkish personality that stood no nonsense from anyone. Mary ruled the roost and even Angie's father, Walter, was wary of her. Angie's brother, Arthur had risen in his world and was managing a motor dealer's near Preston. But Simon was sorry to hear about Mary's stroke. It was right that Angie should go to her at once. Not life-threatening, the report had said, but a stroke was a stroke and not to be trifled with like a sore throat. It really was sad and had put a blight on the family when they had just returned from their best holiday ever. How he recalled holidays in his army days, short breaks and never travelling too far away and subject to recall. Now they had returned from ten idyllic days in the Mediterranean sunshine, days that they would remember all their lives. Then he shut his eyes; he'd had a vision of long ago. Another Mediterranean beach and there was Melina. He saw her lovely slim body, totally nude as she splashed laughing along the shoreline.

Back to work again next morning. Not really a chore. He had arranged for the children to be looked after by a kindly neighbour while he sold one full-size combine harvester to an arable farming company. Fingers crossed he could ensure delivery before the start of harvest. It was good and he felt elated were it not for the news of Angie's mum. Not that there was much news. They had phoned the Bradford hospital and had received a very cryptic report from a nurse with an Indian accent. However it seemed Mary's condition was no worse and by now her daughter should be nearly with her. Angie was due to ring home later that evening.

'Mum's going to be Ok,' Angie's voice came down the phone line. 'She's a bit stiff on her left side and she talks a bit funny, but the doc says with practice and exercise she'll get over it.'

'Thank God for that,' said Simon.

'But she's got to be very careful from now on. You know, take the medicine, eat the right things – do the exercise. If she doesn't next time could be much worse.'

'What about your dad. He's all alone on the farm. Can he cope?'

'Oh yes, the neighbours have been great. They're helping with the milking and all the rest of it.'

'Good, that's real Yorkshire spirit. Although I daresay they'd do the same around here if the farms weren't so big and well staffed.'

'I'm going to stay here for a few more days and then I'll be home. Are the kids all right?'

'They're fine and Hugh and Chris are taking them sailing later.'

'That's lovely. Another week and they'll be back to school. Has Anna been to her music tutor?'

'Yes, she's going there this afternoon. And she's playing in the youth orchestra later this month.'

'She is a little gem. I'm longing for mum and dad to meet her.'

Simon replaced the phone and breathed in his relief. Mary was Ok and that was all that mattered. He was due to visit a farm sixty miles away in Kent, but first he would drop by the photography shop and collect their happy family snaps.

'That's me, that's me,' Anna squeaked as she viewed her photograph. 'And I'm eating that ice cream.'

'They were really yummy,' said Mark.

'Let me see, let me see,' said Lizzie. 'Where's the ones of me in my bikini?'

'They're here,' said her father. 'Vanity; that my girl will be the end of you if you're not careful.'

'Ohoo, it shows my suntan,' said Lizzie. 'I'm all brown. Why wouldn't you take a picture with my top off?'

'Because you are supposed to be becoming a respectable young lady. Not a page three girl!'

'Well you needn't let that Lady Reece what's it see my nice brown titties.'

Simon couldn't help it as his stern demeanour changed to laughter. 'You mean Lady Reece-Lamprey. I don't think we'd ever let the League of Decency see any of your pictures. They, the League, are highly allergic to bare skin.'

'Ha ha,' said Mark as he picked up a picture. 'There's me kicking my football and scoring a goal.'

That evening Simon had spread out the twenty colour pictures on the dining room table. There was a lovely shot of Angie looking so beautiful and tanned; then one of himself, looking a bit corpulent around the tummy.

Lizzie had her mischievous expression. 'Did you take a picture of Auntie Melina?'

'No, I did not.' He pulled a stern fatherly face. Lizzie was not impressed.

Simon put the photographs back in their envelope. 'We've got to look after these for your mother.'

'You do remember I've a music lesson this afternoon?' said Anna.

'Of course I do,' he smiled at her. 'Be ready plus violin and I'll run your there in half an hour.'

Mrs Cangel, the music tutor lived in a house on the outskirts of town not far from the Gladstone's. These private sessions were expensive but neither Simon nor Angie begrudged this. They were doing all they could to help Anna put the past behind her and find a glowing future. Moira Cangel, had played in orchestras until a family of her own had stopped her travelling and she had settle to be a teacher in several local schools including very expensive independent ones.

'We're really pleased with Anna,' said Moira. 'She played the Mozart piece and I found very few faults.'

Simon ruffled his new daughter's hair. 'Don't make her big-headed.'

'I'd have loved to meet Mozart,' said Anna.

Moira burst out laughing. 'Oh, I doubt your mum and dad would approve of that. Mozart was not a role model. He's a complete contradiction. He gave us hours of the most beautiful music, but all accounts at the time say if you met him he was an oik. You know a foul mouthed yob – drink, drugs and girls. Live hard and die young.'

Anna spluttered. 'Lizzie's my sister, she likes the Rolling Stones.'

'Really?' said Moira. 'Well Mozart would probably have felt completely at home with them.'

Simon left Anna and drove home. He wished he had more culture. His knowledge of music was limited and of literature even less.

101

CHAPTER 28

Angie reached Bradford Royal Infirmary and there in the waiting room was her father. She wanted to rush over to embrace and kiss him but that would be very un-Yorkshire. Instead she ran to him and spoke the words that had been in her head for all her trip north.

'Dad, is she all right? Can I see her?'

'Aye, come with me. We've got her in a private room. All that medical insurance I've paid out...'

In spite of everything Angie smiled. Dad was sounding truly Yorkshire.

Her mother was in her room but out of bed and sitting in an armchair. Angie had not known what to expect but she was still shocked. Mum had shrunk; there was no other word for it. She tiptoed across bent down and kissed her.

'Good to see you, Mum. How are you feeling now?' It all sounded very lame.

'Oh Angie, lass. Am I glad you've come. All the way from down South.'

Angie smiled now. 'It's not that far by train. It's not as if I've come from Australia or somewhere.'

'Aye, but them's funny people down there.'

'Not really. We're happy there and Simon's got a really good job.'

'Well, don't either of you forget where you come from.'

Angie was feeling increasingly relieved. Her mother was frail, her speech was slurred but the personality was still there.

'When are we going to see this little girl, Anna? We read all about that evil woman. The trial was in the Daily Mail but we never knew it was you that's rescued the little mite. She's Southern I suppose.'

'No, Anna lost her parents in an air crash. Her mum was American and her dad was Manx.'

'Oh aye. Isle o' Man, well that's sort of Lancashire.'

Angie's father laughed. 'You mustn't say that. Them islanders is a funny lot. I went there once to watch the motor bikes.'

'Anyway,' said Angie. 'Anna is a really lovely little girl. She's settled in with us like she's always been with us and she plays lovely music.'

'Young Simon. Is he behaving?'

'He's being very good and he's earning really good money. We met his fancy girl when we were on holiday in Cyprus. Nothing happened, he's over her, or at least I think he is.'

'You think,' her mother gave a wheezy cackle. 'He's a man. I never trusted 'em.'

You're forgetting your own wartime caper, thought Angie.

'How's your Mark and that Elizabeth?' Mary asked.

Angie told them of Lizzie's school progress. 'She's all set for university and Mark's good at sport. Mum, get well again and we'll all come north to see you. And then, mum you will have to come and stay with us.'

'Hmm, me go south. Never been there. They talks funny and you're beginning to sound that way.'

Angie kissed her mother again. 'Where we live they're all farming folk. Not a lot different to up here.'

'All very well,' said her dad. 'Down south they plays wrong sort o' rugby.'

Outside in the sunlight Angie and her father boarded the family's ancient Landrover and headed for her childhood home in the Dales.

'Lizzie, that poster on your wall. Where did you get that?'

'Oh, Dad, they're printing off thousands of them all over the country. He's Che Guevara. You've gotta' have one of those in your room or you're not cool.'

Simon groaned. 'Lizzie, that man was a far-left extremist, a communist. Given a chance he would have put the likes of me and your Uncle Bill up against a wall and shot us. Then all you young ones would have been slave labour.'

'Yeah, whatever.'

Simon sighed. He knew perfectly well that these fads and fashions were something the youngsters needed to get out of the system before the serious life of work, marriage and children began. Cassandra and Lizzie's local Young Liberals were not to his taste but they were not going to foment revolution. Thank goodness Anna was immersed in her music and Mark in his cricket. Lizzie had a new boyfriend called, Nick. Nick's father was a bank manager and one could hardly be more respectable and middle class than that. Four more days and then the new school term starts. He mustn't revel in the idea of days of peace and quiet. That was unfair. He loved all his three kids and only wanted them to have the best. He was waiting for Angie to ring home with

103

more news of her mother.

At first report it seemed that Mary was well and fighting to recover and better still Angie said she was a her usual grumpy self but with a twinkle.

With the new school term due they had something to cheer about. Lizzie had passed GCE O level in maths, English, biology and physics but had come nowhere in languages.

'They should've had a language paper for speaking Yorkie,' Mark had said cheekily.

'Just you wait,' Lizzie snapped. 'It'll be your turn in a few years.' Simon knew she was worried. It was A Level next and she would need prime results for university entry. Her older friend Cassie was settling into life at Bristol University and had sent a happy letter. She had enthused less about the food, but good lecturers, good research facilities, and of course a wild social life and lots of boys. Lizzie had hidden the letter at first but Mark had found it and shown it to him. Well, Cassie was a bit wild and Lizzie's university time was still some way off.

He had rung Angie at her parent's home. He was told that Angie's mother would be in hospital for another couple of weeks and then she would be allowed home on strict medication supervised by a district nurse. Give her another four days and then Angie would return home to Sussex. She was relieved that her mother's condition had improved but how much farm work she could do was another factor. Angie worried for her father through the coming winter. She thought they might find some casual workers locally but she couldn't ask Arthur, her brother, to abandon his high-salary post to muck out pigs and milk cows. Simon yawned. In another hour he would have to put on a tie brush his hair and go to a meeting of the parish council.

The council chairman held a letter in his hand and he looked gloomy. 'This is a letter of complaint from Lady Reece-Lamprey. She says that our pub, the Windy Ship, has been holding rowdy gatherings on a Friday where indecent songs are sung. Can anyone enlighten us?'

Lucy, the youngest member of the council, smiled. Youngest of course meant she was a thirty-three-year old housewife from the council estate. She was an attractive dark-haired girl and a friend of Angie. 'Friday evening is folk club night. I go to it myself. We have local singers for the first half and then a visiting group for the main show. We pay part of their fee and the pub the rest. As for indecent

songs; the woman's mad.'

Simon knew that the Kellingham family were regulars at this gathering. It wasn't held in the pub bar but in an adjacent annexe. Lizzie had been a couple of times under strict instruction not to accept alcohol and to keep a wary eye on strange men. He guessed she would obey this second instruction to the letter but ignore the first. As far as he knew the entertainment was harmless.

Lucy continued. 'A lot of the songs are traditional. But we sing some big modern names like Ralph McTell. I can't see how that mad woman can complain about his *Streets of London,* it's all about poverty in the working class. I suppose that's why she doesn't like it.'

The chairman smiled. 'She goes on to say that the singing is too loud and it is keeping neighbours awake. Can anyone comment on that?'

Neither of the councillors who lived near the pub reacted to this. 'Very well,' said the chair. 'I will word a tactful reply to Lacy Reece-Lamprey. We have discussed her views but there is nothing we can do to intervene.'

'Tell you something else,' said Lucy. 'Kevin our policeman had been with his wife a few times and he didn't find anything wrong.'

Simon joined in. 'Way back they had the Filthy Swine in the town hall. Her ladyship complained to the town council loud and long about that and she got nowhere.'

Only two days ago there had been a story in the national press and the TV news, how five of Lady R-Ls followers had invaded a London art college waving bed sheets and had tried to cover up the art life models. Apparently the decency protesters had been forcibly ejected and Lady R-L had complained to the Prime Minister. Well, it was a mad world and at least the lady's estate farms were good customers.

CHAPTER 29

Now Angie was home and all three kids were safely back at school. Simon was persuaded, reluctantly, to get up in the morning at seven a.m. to take Lonny the Labrador for a walk. In holiday time and at half-term this was the children's duty and Anna's in particular. Lonny was elderly but he could still jump up and try and lick Simon's face.

This additional member of the family had been an overwhelming success. He was Anna's special friend and was so important in replacing the memory of her murdered cat. Lonny followed the girl around and often slept on her bunk bed at night. Simon wondered how they both found room to move. He had suffered all his married life from a wife who rolled around in her sleep and tried to push him out of what he regarded as his allotted space. That had never happened with Melina, but no, he mustn't think about her. He attached the dog lead to Lonny's collar, picked up the much chewed tennis ball and left the house.

It was a beautiful September morning and they set off on the quarter of a mile to Shinkley Woods, the very place where Lizzie and Mark had first seen Anna. A Rolls-Royce filling the entire width of the lane cruised by. In the back was the portly figure of Rufus Blanner. The man looked out, clearly recognised Simon and glared. Simon resisted the schoolboy urge to put up two fingers.

He found the wood a magical place as had his children. He had grown up near the seaside town of Whitby, a great place to spend childhood with its steep hillsides, little harbour and ruined abbey. In a different way this was just as good. The children could imagine robbers and ghosts, until like Mark and Lizzie they had seen Anna; an event that had changed all their lives for the better. The foliage overhead and the thick undergrowth to each side of the path reminded him of his days on field exercises. For hours his platoon and he had searched for elusive special-forces men who somehow had discovered invisibility. On a whim he called the dog to him and branched right off the path into the brambles and long grass. Lonny followed with a yelp of pleasure and started to sniff rabbit trails. For ten minutes Simon pushed on through the undergrowth until unexpectedly the trees ended and he saw sunlight and blue sky. A few yards further forward and he

was standing on the edge of an almost vertical slope covered in short scrub bushes. There far below on the flat ground was a substantial house beside a lane. The trouble was he knew that house with its short drive and heavy iron gates; and there beside the gates were the two flagpoles with a union flag and another, the ensign of the BPP. So, Shinkley's other mad commune was still active. He turned as he heard a snap of broken twigs. Standing a few yards away was a figure wearing military fatigues, a woollen hat and a black full-face mask with eyeholes. Whoever this apparition was he was never a real soldier. He was visibly obese and breathing heavily.

Simon fixed the man with a glare and addressed him in his best parade ground tone. 'You don't look a soldier to me. I suppose you're a follower of Wally Fircomb. I understand he's discovered God.' The man began to wave a gun around: an obviously fake Kalashnikov, a theatrical prop for certain.

'I know you,' the man spoke with a London accent. 'Seen you around. You works for that black bastard Gladstone. Ain't a decent white boss good enough?'

'I'm not arguing with you. What's your game up here anyway?'

'We're training for the day.'

Simon fumed. 'What day?'

'The day our new leader will take over the nation. The day we'll throw out all the darkies, Pakkies, Paddies and Yids. We'll shoot the politicians and hang that bugger Fircomb from our flagpole down there.' The man gesticulated down the hill to the house below.

Behind him came a crashing in the undergrowth and Lonny broke into sight. The BBP man reacted. He retreated and nearly tripped over backwards. 'That your dog,' he yelled. 'Get it off. Get it away from me!' The supposed bold soldier was clearly terrified.

Lonny sensed this and crouched growling with menace. The BPP man had had enough, he turned and ran, crashing through the scrub and bushes while glancing every so often behind him. Lonny made no move to follow but loped over to where Simon stood and sat down. Simon felt a wave of affection for the old pooch. 'Oh, Lonny, good fellow. You saw him off good and true.' Yes, he thought so these were the brave revolutionaries who would take over the nation. He looked at his watch. Well, it was time to take Lonny home and get the car on the road.

Simon returned home that evening. He had had a modestly successful day, managing to interest customers in new equipment but not

managing to complete a sale. He had remained distracted by that weird encounter with the BPP. He was both amused and angry. The idea of a Neo-Nazi takeover was absurd, just as the cowardly BPP soldier that morning was absurd. But he was also angry. His father and Angie's father had both fought against Hitler. His father had been wounded and had never recovered the use of one arm. He didn't talk much about those times. He had seen friends and comrades gunned down.

As Simon walked through the front to door he heard Anna's violin. Now he froze. She was playing a tune that he had heard before played by his regimental band. It took him straight back to another sunny day. That time on the parade ground in front of his whole battalion, his wife, tiny daughter, Lizzie and baby Mark. The sun had shone down as he marched forward to salute the general who had pinned on his tunic the Military Cross. All the while the band had played and they had played Anna's tune. He tiptoed into the sitting room but Anna saw him and put down her instrument to give Lonny a hug.

'Oh, Anna, don't stop, but that tune. What is it?'

She smiled. 'It's Handel – "where'er you walk". It's lovely and I'm playing it with our orchestra next month. We've got a famous tenor coming down to sing it.'

'Well, love, rely on us; we'll all be there to listen to you.'

'Where do you keep your medal?' asked Angie who had come into the room.

'It's in the top drawer of my desk. So, you remember that tune.'

'Of course I do, we'll never forget that day. Anyway my family were bonkers about Handel. They all sang in choral societies.'

Simon hadn't wanted to boast of his alleged gallantry. He could barely remember the details of the incident in Cyprus. The day they had been ambushed on patrol and he had risked himself to help three wounded comrades out of the line of fire. He had then rallied his patrol and driven off the ambushers. The reality had set in later that evening when he had sneaked out of camp and snuggled up to Melina in her bedsit flat. But he mustn't think of her. Forget her, but he couldn't.

'It's Remembrance Day in a few weeks,' said Angie. 'You must wear it then by the village war memorial. I told the committee about your medal and they suggested you read the dedication. It always used to be Rufus Blanner doing it but he's a bit groggy on his feet apparently.'

'I don't want to offend him,' Simon was worried. Blanner was a

pompous idiot but he had won his MC going over the top at the Somme. Simon could hardly match that.

'You won't offend anyone. They were delighted to hear about your medal. You know everyone likes you around here.'

CHAPTER 30

It was September, the month when most of the harvest was already gathered and the autumn ploughing and seeding had begun. Simon loved this time of year. Winter was still some weeks away and the countryside looked at its best. It was a delight to smell the scent of newly-turned earth and watch the gulls chasing the ploughs to pick up discarded seeds of barley. It wasn't without problems. A new seed drill imported from Germany was causing him grief on one estate. It had some sort of revolutionary electronic control system for distributing the seed and it didn't work. Finally it had to be withdrawn to the Gladstone workshop and replaced with a conventional wheel driven version.

Simon had had a call to the new winery. It was a chance to sell a small tractor but he knew that Melina had twice called there recently selling wine vats and he didn't want to see her. Angie would not be so forgiving this time if he did. In fact the coast was clear. He sold the tractor and a small trailer made for grape boxes. The annual grape harvest was due and this would speed it when the time came.

For a year now Angie, Lizzie as well as Cassie Kellingham had been ranting about the war in Vietnam. Simon agreed that the American position was dubious. He was thankful that he and his comrades had never had to serve in a miserable mismanaged campaign like this one. The final American defeat seemed meant, and oddly was a big relief. Contrary to everything that had been said in propaganda the defeat had not resulted in a domino effect flooding the world with red revolution. Thank goodness that was about all the politics flowing around Shinkley right now. Sussex seemed insulated from all the talk of unrest and strikes that sensationalised the media. Poor Jill Hilldown was already on the wrong side of Margaret Thatcher and her party advancement stalled. Bill, who was a yachting friend of Edward Heath, was talking of putting more finance into the local Liberal party although even Hugh Kellingham agreed there was nil chance of unseating Thatcher's Tories in a main election. Anyway this was a world that Simon was still not fond of. He determined to keep his head down and do his job.

At least his family news was happier. Angie's mother was not only

110

home but was beginning to walk with the aid of elbow crutches. She had flatly refused the offer of a wheelchair. She had taken over all the record keeping on the farm leaving Angie's father free to do the manual work with the dairy herd. Arthur, Angie's bother had travelled twice from Preston to help on the farm.

Lizzie, thank goodness was working hard with her A Levels and next term both Mark and Anna would be joining her at the comprehensive school. It had been a difficult search with some detective work tracing birth records as far as the Isle of Man. It was a shock to discover that Anna would also be age thirteen in May. Simon had not thought she was much more then ten. In three weeks' time the whole family would go to the Memorial Theatre to hear and see Anna play in the youth orchestra.

The next day Simon had taken an afternoon off. He was not due for a fun time but for a dental appointment. This was a routine visit at a practice in the town. It was a painful occasion, but as the alleged gallant soldier he had to grin and bear it as the saying went.

He wasn't too sure whether he wasn't being singled out by the prejudice of Mike O'Carrigan the dentist. Mike was a cheerful Irishman from Northern Ireland and a republican. He insisted he was wholly against the violence there, but he resented the presence of the British army. Simon suspected he personally was being blamed for this. For himself he was relieved that he had left the army before his regiment had been deployed near Belfast. This was politics again and typically the politicians were hiding behind the army. The arguments had intruded a little into their own locality. Rufus Blanner had written to the local paper. He called for mass arrests of suspected sympathisers even here in Sussex. Hugh Kellingham had taken the line: "can't win then give in". Simon was utterly opposed to both these attitudes but couldn't think of a sensible way out. So far there had been no casualties among his former comrades but it was a worry.

Mike the dentist shone his light into Simon's mouth. 'Can't do much with that tooth. It's chipped and decayed and you say it hurts.'

'Not all the time, but it can ache like hell at night.'

'Right, I advise out it and we'll give you a nice dental plate to keep your beauty.'

'What'll that cost?' Simon was more worried about the bill than the pain.

Mike gave him a suggested price and Simon winced. 'You'd better do it. What about a pain killer?'

The dentist grinned a tad sadistically. 'My old dad was a wartime dentist in Belfast. He once had to pull out teeth of six Russian sailors. They didn't want any pain killers. You Brits are soft.'

'Well I do want it and I am definitely not a sailor or a Russian.'

The day had come. Anna was to play that evening with the county youth orchestra in the Memorial Theatre. The concert was due to start at eight o'clock, but Moira, Anna's tutor had fetched the girl a couple of hours earlier. 'Has Anna told you about her part tonight?' asked Moira.

Angie looked puzzled. 'I know she's in the violins.'

Moira smiled. 'Then she hasn't told you – good.'

They left and Anna blew her family a kiss.

'What do we make of that?' said Simon.

'Anna is more nervous than I expected but it's a big occasion.'

'Tammie Kellingham knows something secret, but she wouldn't tell me,' said Mark.

'Never mind,' said Simon. 'We'd better all get changed and look respectable.'

They reached the theatre at a little after seven thirty. The premises had a vast car park, much needed as the theatre was the venue for famous names and pre-West End runs. It was pleasing to see it filling up well for tonight's show. The building contained a restaurant where they had booked for a post-performance meal and a large entrance hall with a bar. Simon bought Angie and himself glasses of wine and Mark and Lizzie orange juice. They waved to the Kellingham clan across the hall and to several others that they knew.

The Kellinghams joined them. 'They're selling programmes over there,' said Christine pointing to a long table.

'Thanks,' replied Simon. He walked across and bought three copies. The programmes were well produced and illustrated with adverts from local shops and companies including Gladstone Engineering. Inside were the performance list and the name and photograph of the conductor. Then he stopped still and stared at anther quarter page photograph. *Orchestra Leader: Miss Anna Robsby.* Simon almost ran across to his family.

'Hey, look at this.'

'Well, well,' said Angie. 'So that's Anna's secret. We never knew.'

'We did,' said Christine. 'In fact all my lot knew. Moira the teacher said that Anna is so advanced; they couldn't not give her the job when

the other leader left.'

'But she's only just thirteen,' said Angie.

'That's nothing this band has an upper age limit of sixteen. Then they move to the main Southern Youth Orchestra and possibly to one of the big London ones after that.'

'Oh, well done Anna. What a talent,' said Simon.

Cassandra stared at him. 'Why are you talking funny?'

'Cassie,' said her mother. 'That was rather rude don't you think.'

Simon grinned. 'The blooming dentist has sabotaged my front teeth.'

He looked at the programme. Part One contained the Handel's Semele, whatever that meant. Then a piano concerto Rachmaninov Two. Simon wished he knew more about serious music. Part Two of the concert was wholly devoted to music with a Sussex flavour. Eric Coates', the Merry Makers. Adinsell's Warsaw Concerto; he knew that one, played by the same boy talent. Last of all the programme listed Movement three of the War Symphony. He marvelled that this iconic work could be within the capability of a youth orchestra. It was Colonel Cohen's favourite and often heard on the record player in the officer's mess. It was haunting and hypnotic. He understood it had been composed by a musician from Sussex who had been a Battle of Britain fighter pilot. That was about all he knew.

It was time to find their seats. It was the first time he had been in this auditorium and he was impressed. The seating was a half-moon with a low projecting stage fully set with music stands. The young players filed into their places. The lights dimmed and then a special moment as the leader, their own Anna entered to loud applause. She smiled and bowed. Finally the adult conductor entered to more applause. The music began with the Handel *Where'ere you walk* sung by a fine adult tenor. Once again Simon was taken back to the medal award day. The sixteen-year-old pianist played Rachmaninov with a panache well in advance of his years. Of course, this was the theme for the film Brief Encounter. Simon had known his own brief encounter with Melina. No, he really must stop thinking about her.

Now there was an interval. Along with most of the audience they walked down into the foyer and Simon bought more drinks all round. Anna was waving from the stage door and they hurried across to her. Her new family kissed and congratulated her. An electric bell rang and it was time to resume their seats for the rest of the concert and the

famous War Symphony.[1]

As the last movement opened Simon marvelled at the ability of these tiny tots to grasp this sophisticated music; some of the most iconic to have emerged in the aftermath of World War Two. Played by a full orchestra this was a different experience to listening to a vinyl recording. This was music that made you stop in your tracks. Music that made you put down a book stop reading a newspaper, pause eating food. It really did convey the listener back to those terrible times. Simon knew the work had been inspired by the composer seeing a friend die in battle. This he could understand. These children playing could not – hopefully they never would. The end of the work was built around a diminuendo; Simon thought that was the right term. But it was hypnotic. An orchestra all in close harmony playing a single theme loudly, then fading quieter and quieter with that enigma that echoed the bugle: *sunset call* that he so well remembered. He glanced at his own family. Lizzie was motionless her mouth open and there were tears running down her face. Yes, this was music of power and pathos; ten million miles from the likes of the Filthy Swine.

---

[1] For an explanation of the War Symphony see *Song of Sussex* by James Morley.

CHAPTER 31

The whole family had been moved by the youth concert and Anna's key part in it. For Anna herself it was a boost of self-confidence that was cathartic. She stopped having bouts of depression, fewer nightmares and terrifying returns to her past at the hands of the Shartcroft. Young as she was she knew her future and was determined to achieve it. It was October now and soon there would be Christmas. Simon could only marvel at his and his family's good fortune since he had made his life-changing decision to quit the army. It was all so contradictory: a Yorkshireman in Southern England, he had found this secure job with a friendly employer and he had settled in Shinkley Common, a bizarre and interesting place gripped by its eccentric inhabitants. Then a family of four had gained another member. An unhappy abused child had emerged as a talented musician with a good future. Yes, they were luckier than they deserved.

Now was the time to plan the family's trip north to see Angie's mother. The local schools had a break coming up and this would be the ideal time. The children had grown since their grandparents had last seen them and it was time to introduce the new member of the family. Anna could still practice her music and it seemed her orchestra had no more formal concerts until Christmas.

Simon examined the road map. 'I think we should do this trip in two stages. A drive that long in one go would tire the kids.'

'Agreed,' replied Angie. 'I don't want you falling asleep at the wheel either.'

'Right, straight up the M1 and then we branch off and stay the night at this hotel that Bill Gladstone had got a share in. That means as an employee we'll get a good discount.'

Angie smiled. 'Good man, spoken like a true Yorkie. Save the pennies.'

That morning Simon had a call from Carl Mortlish, Lady Reece-Lamprey's estate manager. The estate was interested in buying a small tractor for working with the livestock. Simon arrived at the estate office and what he saw made his heart sink. There stood a horse and beside the horse dressed in riding breeches stood the dumpy figure of

the lady herself. He had never met her in person for all the months he had had dealings with her farms. But he did remember her long irrational rant at the town hall meeting and her nationwide reputation. There was no alternative and frankly he was interested as he strode to her and explained who he was.

'Oh, of course,' she replied. 'You work for William.'

'Bill Gladstone, yes I'm his salesman.'

'Indeed, we like William. Do you realise he and his family are devout Catholics?'

Well, yes, Simon knew that although he wasn't too sure how devout the family were.

'Now, Mr Robsby. Yesterday was Sunday. Did you attend church?'

Fortunately he didn't have to lie. 'Yes, we all went to our family's Methodist chapel.'

Well, that was true but the motive was to hear Anna accompany hymns with her violin. The Minister had congratulated her.

'That is good,' said Lady R-L. 'I hope you gained spiritual succour and will put that to maintaining purity of morals.'

Oh, why was he thinking of Melina again? He had a sudden vision of her lovely suntanned naked body. Behind Lady R-L's back Carl pulled a wry face.

Now the lady actually smiled, then climbed aboard her patient horse and moved off out of the yard.

'Simon, sorry about all that,' said Carl. 'The old girl does go on a bit, but really she's got a good heart.'

'Well, I'm glad I've met her. Quite a personality there. Now, what about a tractor?'

A puzzling encounter ended with the signing of the deal for a new medium horsepower two-wheel drive tractor. He drove back to the office with the paperwork. Why on earth was Shinkley the abode of so much oddity all clustered in one small village? He couldn't really blamed this on southern culture when it was likely a similar colony of loonies existed somewhere in the north. Tomorrow they would begin the family's long drive northwards. Now why did he start thinking about it as some ordeal or adventure? They were travelling a mere two hundred miles to his and Angie's home country to see their own flesh and blood.

The Rover packed with Simon, wife, children, gifts and overnight bags hummed north up the M1. They had started early and until they

reached the height of the rush hour it had been an easy ride. Short of Birmingham they had branched off to find the isolated and peaceful Gladstone company hotel. This was the second time that Simon had stayed here. The first being the conference visit to Birmingham with Bill. He could not easily forget that time and their encounter with the offensive racist policeman. The hotel only a few miles from the great city was a delight. It had an extensive garden with swings and slides for the children and to their disappointment a swimming pool closed and empty for the winter.

A good evening meal, a night's sleep, then breakfast and they were on their way again. Simon made good time past Bradford and on to Harrogate. Sitting beside him Angie checked the road map. 'You know,' she said. 'It's only since we moved south that I've noticed the name clashes. For God's sake this is Yorkshire and here we have places called Ripley and Farnham.'

'I dunno', said Simon. 'I think the Angles and Saxons got around a bit. In my parts up by Whitby, we're all Vikings.'

Angie laughed. 'I know. Vikings – arson, rape and pillage is what you lot got up to.'

'Much less these days I hope.'

It was early afternoon when they reached the Leacrum's family farm a few miles north of Harrogate. This was Nidderdale, a beautiful country of trees and rolling hills and, Simon had to admit, not so very different from Sussex. The family's farmhouse was a substantial stone-built home surrounded by traditional stone barns and a modern steel span cow yard. Angie left the car and ran across the forecourt as if she was a schoolgirl again. The children followed while Simon parked the Rover out of the way of any tractors.

Simon was pleasantly surprised to see the first figure to greet them was Angie's brother, Arthur. Today Arthur, the young business executive, was dressed in dungarees and Wellington boots. 'I've got ten days off,' he said, 'so I'm giving a hand on the farm and I must say I'm enjoying it.'

Next out of the house came Angie's father, Walter. It was a few years since Simon had last seen Walter but the man had hardly aged. 'Aye, good to see you, young Simon.'

'Very pleased to see you, Walter, but how's Mary?'

'She's getting along now. Still uses them crutches but she's mending. Doc says she's got to take life a bit steady for a while.'

Now Simon saw Mary. She had emerged from the house and was clipping along on her elbow crutches smiling broadly. 'Simon, lad,

good to see you again and my how those kids o' yours have grown. I like the little girl you've taken in, but by gum she talks very southern. You're not catching that yourself I hope. I've just spoken to my Ange and she's taken a bit of a posh south to her tongue.'

Simon shook the hand that Mary had released from her right crutch. 'Anna's been brought up in the South, but actually she's Manx with an American mum.'

'Aye, I know. Angie told us and we read in the papers all about that bloody murdering aunt and the poor little puss. They should've put that evil one away for ten year.'

'Anyway, mum, how are you making out? We had a nasty shock when we heard you'd been taken sick.'

Mary grinned. 'Oh, I'm a bit shaky on the pins but I'm on the mend.'

Walter called. 'Come in all o'you. Have a cuppa tea. You've come a good long way.'

The strong brew tea was just what they needed. 'Right,' said Walter. 'How's life away from t'army?'

Simon expected this. 'Walter, it's fine. We may be in the south now, but it's good. My new job's interesting and the pay's good.'

'Aye, lad. We're proud of you. Army major you were. I only made it to sergeant.'

'Sure, but you won the war for us.'

Mary cackled. 'Did he do that in a Naples whore house?'

Simon couldn't help but laugh. 'R and R we call it. You know rest and recreation. Without that we couldn't have won the war.'

'Hmm, men,' grunted Mary.

'Wasn't much fun and games in Catterick when I did national service,' said Arthur.

'Aye, son,' said Mary, 'I wager you found some any road. What about you, Simon?'

'What about me?'

There came a splutter of laughter from Lizzie. 'We met dad's fancy girl when we went to Cyprus.'

'Lizzie!' Angie roared. 'That's out of order. You apologise. Now!'

'Well, it's true. She was nice and she found us a nice place to stay.'

'Didn't find a nice bed as well?' laughed Mary. 'Liz, watch out for men. Don't trust any o'em out of your sight.'

'I know,' said Lizzie. 'My boy friend, he's ex now, is a snake in the grass.'

'Which one?' asked Simon. He was really more amused than angry

about Lizzie's reference to Melina. 'I'd better explain. Lizzie is by way of being our school's local femme fatale.'

'Well, why not?' said Mary as she grinned at her granddaughter. 'Make hay while t'sun shines I say.'

Yes, mother dear, thought Angie. Do you think I was too young to remember Uncle Stefan in the war? And why was he always still here at breakfast time next morning?

CHAPTER 32

The children had a happy three days exploring the farm, watching the milking and stroking and talking to the cows. Angie was worried as to how Dad would cope with the extra work once Arthur had gone back to Preston.

'Oh. Don't worry your head about me, lass. The NFU have found me a couple of student lads and a girl to help out. One o' the lads is a good milker and likes the cows.'

'And Dad, mum's got to come south and stay with us sometime. Can't you persuade her?'

'Aye, she's a bit funny about Southerners but she'll make the trip all right. I can't leave t' farm but she can.'

'It'll only be for a week and the people in Sussex are no different to those here.'

'What about t'mad bitch that ill-treated little Anna?'

'Yes, Dad. The woman was crazy but she wasn't from Sussex. She was an American and is back there for good now.'

Sadly it was time for the family to say goodbye and head for home. It had been so good seeing Walter, Mary and Arthur again and to witness Mary's amazing post stroke recovery. The children would never forget the farm and getting to know their grandparents and uncle. It was a fine autumn morning but still dark when they departed heading south. This time Simon did the trip in one hop and in the late afternoon they reached home.

One hundred Shinkley villagers plus visiting relatives stood by the village war memorial. The church clock struck eleven times. The assembly stood. heads bowed for the two minutes. For Simon who had seen so much in his short life this was one of his proudest moments. Wearing his best suit and his Military Cross he stood beside the vicar and spoke the words:

> *'They grow not old as we who are left grow old*
> *Age shall not weary them nor the years condemn*
> *At the going down of the sun*
> *And in the morning*
> *We will remember them'.*

Traditionally Shinkley's dedication had been spoken by Rufus Blanner. This year the old man had been laid flat with some disorder, most people thought advanced gout, and he could not be present. Simon had been everyone's choice to speak the words at the ceremony. He felt warmth and a deep affection for this community. Three years ago he had arrived, a stranger, an outsider and they had accepted him. So much had happened along the way but this was his home now and his family's. He would live and die in Shinkley and be buried in the churchyard beside which he stood this day.

It wasn't just that his background was military, but so many of those around him at this ceremony had seen real horrors: bomber crews who had lost almost all their comrades, Far East prisoners of war, sailors from Arctic convoys, Dunkirk veterans and many more who had had experiences he could hardly comprehend. His daughter Lizzie had complained at being dragged to this ceremony. "I'm against war", she had shouted. Well, not half as much against war as these men and women standing here who had witnessed war first hand. He had recently learned that Bill, his employer, had been landed in France not long after D Day as a captain in R.E.M.E, the mechanical engineers, and that Bill had been one of only a handful of black commissioned officers in the whole allied armed forces. Bill's company through the rest of the war had repaired vehicles and tanks, often while under fire. He had learned from Bill's wife that her husband was also a holder of the Military Cross. It all made his, Simon's war seem rather trivial.

Now it was Christmas again. Oh, how quickly the months had spun by. The children were a whole year older if not that wiser. Mark had already entered the senior school where his sister was working for her A Levels. Lizzie, thank goodness was working hard at her studies although she had discarded yet another boyfriend. Simon and Angie had met Lizzie's form tutor. This lady was anxious that the girl should set her sights on Oxbridge. Simon could not quite get his head around this news. Oxford or Cambridge was an ambition far beyond anything the family had achieved. Simon's own selection for Sandhurst all those years ago had surprised his family. What would they think of Lizzie aiming for such exalted seats of learning?

Anna's ambitions were easier to comprehend. Both her school and private tutors were certain that Anna would win a place in the Royal College of Music. Her violin playing had progressed to the point

where she could play concertos with her youth orchestra and a few weeks ago she had played *The Lark Ascending* by Vaughn-Williams at a special concert in the Cathedral. Anna still had occasional nightmares, but memories of her birth parents and then her abuse by the evil Shartcroft had faded. She accepted and was happy to be a Robsby.

Lizzie had had a ticking off from her mother. The girl had picked up the rumour that they had all heard already. Cassandra Kellingham had got herself pregnant at university and had had a termination; so much for reasoned argument and relevant awareness. The Kellingham parents had not spoken of this event and Lizzie should not be finding it funny. It was more amusing to speculate about the children of the girls on the Blanner estate and wonder who their same father might be.

This was all getting dangerously close to politics again. The Wilson government was bent on holding a referendum next year on their new terms of membership of the Common Market. This was exciting both Rufus Blanner and Hugh Kellingham from opposite ends of the argument. Simon didn't feel he could share either old man Blanner's hatred of foreigners or Hugh's internationalism. Bill Gladstone worried that withdrawal from the market might damage farm machinery sales. Gladstone Machinery had a sister company in Holland and mutual trade had increased. For example the vine sprayers were made in Germany as were many other pieces of equipment. Vineyard gear, hell! Now, once again he saw that picture in his mind of Melina naked and smiling at him.

Whatever he might think, politics was intruding more and more. The national inflation rate was somewhere around twenty percent. Not bad if one had a stable bank overdraft but a disaster for the national economy. Petrol at the little garage in Shinkley had almost doubled in price in three months. Even the subsidised farm diesel fuel was rocketing in price. Farmers grumbled from habit but now they had a reason. Everyone blamed the Wilson government but Simon was unsure if a conservative administration would be able to hold back the tide of gloom. He and the family was on good terms with Jill, the local MP. Jill was worried that although her party had a woman leader for the first time, Thatcher was wholly unsympathetic to the cause of her own gender. Stef and Tess in the village feminist commune were hostile to the lady and felt let down. Anyway the nearest Simon got to politics were the monthly parish council meetings. Legend said that great political decisions were always taken in smoke-filled rooms. Shinkley Parish Council took no great decisions of any kind but met in

a chain smokers' paradise. Simon had experimented with smoking as a schoolboy and hated it. Now he had to go to these meetings in a fog of tobacco haze and watch some of his fellows destroy their lungs.

Christmas was once again a special time for the family. At least Lizzie would no longer demand a Christmas stocking. The other two kids would certainly still want theirs. Simon knew he and Angie together were now well enough off to buy generous presents for all. In anticipation of the day Simon had approached a famous cricket bat maker and ordered a special made-to-measure bat for Mark. Angie had bought Lizzie a beautiful pale blue sun dress for wearing next year and an expensive hand bag. He had bought her a course of driving lessons. Anna already had her violin from last year and loved it. She had had her bicycle for her last birthday. Then Simon had seen a miniature piano, with a brand new type electronic system, that would fit nicely in the corner of a room. It was expensive but Anna was their pride and joy and she was worth it.

Simon looked up from his desk. 'Lizzie, where's your mum?'

'She's gone to the doctor. She's got some tummy trouble again.'

'Just as well get it sorted or it'll spoil her Christmas.'

'That's her back now,' said Lizzie. Yes, he could hear her car pull into the drive.

Minutes later Angie was in the house. She had an odd expression as she stared at him. 'Know what?' she said.

'All right, what?'

'I've been to the doctor. I'm pregnant.'

CHAPTER 33

Simon felt his jaw sag open as he stiffened with real shock. 'But you can't be. You're well over forty.'

'Doctor made all the tests. Says I'm right on the age limit but still fertile.'

'But when, how?'

'Seems it was six weeks ago,' Angie grinned at him. 'Come on, do try and look a bit more pleased. This is something special.'

'But when? I don't remember.'

'Well, I do. It was six weeks ago as I said. I knew I was on the edge of my month but I thought it was still Ok.' This time she glared. 'Oh, yes. Have you been busy elsewhere? I had a letter that you never saw.'

'What letter?' Simon's head was in a whirl now and Angie was still looked at him with that mocking glare.

'Two days ago. You left for work early and weren't here when the postman came. He had a letter with a Cyprus stamp. As I said; have you been busy?'

'Busy?'

'Yes, Melina wrote. She's expecting a baby.'

Simon reacted. 'Now, you look here. I haven't seen Melina since we left Cyprus...'

'Yes, all right. I know and the dates don't add up. You quite sure you didn't have a sneaky cuddle with her at that winery?'

'I tell you, I haven't seen sight nor sound of Melina since we came back from Cyprus.'

'All right, all right, will you calm down. As it happens this time I think I actually believe you.'

Simon relaxed and then stood up and kissed his wife, 'I'm sorry I asked questions, but this is great news.'

'I know. I'm just coming to terms with it and I'm excited. Doctor says I've got to take life very easy and not drink a drop of alcohol. Then if all goes well, we'll have another little mouth to feed in June or July time.'

Simon was thinking ahead. 'What do we tell the children?'

'I think we should be straight with them Tell them the news now.'

In the end the three children greeted the news almost with indifference. The future arrival of a sibling was it seemed a non-event. Well, they would all see how they felt when the day came. The months ahead would certainly be an ordeal. Angie was committed to a very relaxed life style, with careful eating and no alcohol and regular medical checks. The doctor said she was not unique and he had had other patients who had delivered healthy babies when in their forties and one even older. To Simon this was only partly reassuring. What if his beloved wife were unable to deliver the child and it died? What if she died? The thought filled him with horror and desolation that he could not face. Once again as it had been in the army under fire, he prayed.

Simon would let nothing spoil the family Christmas. He had bought presents for all, including a modern coffee maker for Angie. He wasn't sure that coffee was allowed and hinted that he might go out and buy an adjustable easy chair. This suggestion had nearly moved his wife to give him a slap. Yes, she would follow doctor's orders but would not allow these to over intrude on her daily life.

A special moment came two days later when the whole family drove the few miles north and across the border into Hampshire. Here, in the Petersfield concert hall they sat and listened to Anna playing *The Lark Ascending,* backed by her youth orchestra. A young girl playing sophisticated music; the audience had loved it. The programme notes, thankfully, had not mentioned anything about her family background and Simon wondered how many present connected her with the little girl in the Shartcroft trial. He had worried that Anna's success with her music might arouse jealousy with the other two but not so. They were not musical but had their own ambitions. Mark was set, he hoped, to be a top sportsman and Lizzie to be some sort of scientist. Most important Anna herself had developed no conceit from her success. She seemed to have sense of predestination. She knew she was going to be a top rank artist and would contain her ego.

'Angie, you mustn't do that. What if you slipped and fell?' Simon had found his wife decorating the Christmas tree standing on a small set of collapsible steps.

'Oh do belt up, I'm not going to slip and fall and anyway it'll be months before I have to slow down and stop doing things.'

'I still don't like it. I mean can you feel anything happening?'

'Oh look, there's nothing yet to feel. There's only a tiny blob in my womb – it'll be weeks before it starts kicking. Bloody men!'

'You sound like the Shartcroft.'

Angie climbed off the steps and turned. She had a sad expression now. 'You know I can feel almost sorry for her...'

'Well, I can't, not after all she did to Anna and burning that poor cat to death.'

'Yes, I know, but her hatred of men is such that she'll never have a child or know what it means.'

'Good thing, as far as I'm concerned.'

On Christmas Eve, Simon filled the two kids' stockings and Angie laid out the wrapped presents under the tree. They couldn't very well conceal Anna's mini-piano so she had been given it a few hours early. Delighted, she had sat before the keyboard and rapidly showed a talent for that instrument as well as her violin. They were determined to make this day even more special. Next Christmas if all went well they would have an extra family member. So, on Christmas morning it was up early and down the road to chapel.

They spent a happy hour singing carols and then returning home to enjoy presents and a massive turkey dinner. Simon opened a new case of local wine and the children were all allowed a sip which they didn't much care for. The next morning they awoke to the distant hallooing of the Blanner Fox Hounds doing their Boxing Day chase. Simon was indifferent to this country custom although the female members of the family were utterly opposed to it. As far as Simon could discover, this Boxing Day hunt was a sort of Southern social ritual and few foxes were ever killed. The long weekend concluded with the Monday bank holiday and then it was return to work on Tuesday for the parents while the children were offloaded into the care of Christine Kellingham.

The Kellighams of course were full of the worsening political situation. The daily talk of strikes and disruption was filling newspapers and TV news bulletins. This hardly affected the pace of life in Shinkley although Rufus Blanner had called for a military coup to take over government, echoing a similar call from the BPP. For Simon this was a quiet time on the big arable estates so he didn't expect much trade. Now it was the long weekend and the beginning of a new year. It would be 1976 and come next August they would have been in Shinkley for three years. So much had happened: a new home, a good

job, and a talented new member of the family. Now there was hope of yet another new member, boy or girl, he couldn't decide which he would prefer. Fate would reveal all in good time.

All the family were allowed to watch the New Year in on television. Despite the dismal national outlook the crowds were the same and the fireworks spectacular. The whole household stood as Anna played the national anthem on her new piano, although no one risked trying to sing it. Then a winter gale swept over the country doing some damage and removing the weathercock from Shinkley church spire.

'I'm not going up there to put it back,' said Lizzie. 'I hate heights.'

'I don't mind,' said Mark.

'I think,' said Angie. 'That this time we'll leave it to the professionals.'

'What, the lot on that TV show? Shouldn't think they'd be much use.'

CHAPTER 34

In May the district went to the polls for the county election. In the Shinkley and district Hugh Kellingham topped the poll for the seat on the West Sussex council. This time Simon and Angie had voted for their friend with genuine enthusiasm. Rufus Blanner's Tory nominee had been badly defeated and Blanner had stalked out of the count shouting abuse. The whole family had sat around the television that Saturday when south coast Southampton had defeated Manchester United at Wembley in the FA Cup. Simon as a Yorkshire man had no high opinion of Manchester and had been happy to share some of his community's pleasure in putting one over the North.

The weather was causing surprise. A freak summer heatwave that was to last for many weeks was bringing temperatures that would rival the Mediterranean. Simon was increasingly fed up with sweating around his sales contacts dressed in a dark suit with collar and tie. As the weeks went by he discarded this outfit for cooler casual wear and nobody seemed to notice. The girls in his family began to adopt dress that was not only casual but far too revealing in his opinion. He had shouted at Lizzie when she had gone down to the roadside topless in that next-to-nothing bikini. She had grinned back at him and told him the Kellingham kids were running around naked again. 'Well. Don't you join them or your mother'll have something to say and so will I.' A pretty empty threat that one, he mused. He had to admit he loved to see his wife, suntanned in her halter-top backless sun dress. Little Anna had a more demure dress in a similar style.

Mark was obsessed with his cricket and had become the youngest member of a successful village team. He had attracted the attention of a county selector while Anna had continued playing local concerts and impressing professional musicians. She was destined for the Royal College of Music even though the prospect was a trifle daunting. Anna still felt wary of the outside world and didn't welcome having to leave her secure new family and make do in London. Anyway that would be a few years yet when she had reached age eighteen.

Simon kept a worried but wary eye on Angie. He knew better than to fuss around her and ask questions about "your condition". His wife seemed very happy at the prospect of another child. He knew it would

still be a few weeks before she showed advanced physical signs. No, he must not fuss. Angie knew how to look after herself. He only wished the rest of the family would be more excited about the birth of a brother or sister to them.

That Monday Simon made a routine monthly call to Solvington Estate. In the farm office, to his amused horror, he found Lady Reece-Lamprey sifting through accounts with Carl Mortlish. Her ladyship gave him a dazzling smile that somewhat confused Simon until she explained. 'Oh, you are Mr Robsby who rescued that poor little girl from those delusional women.'

'Little Anna, yes, we've adopted her now.'

'You are to be congratulated. I have heard good things. You attend the Methodist chapel in your village and the child is good at music.'

Simon didn't know what to say. 'Yes, Anna is on her way to being a good musician.'

'I hope very much she will be playing music of taste and good morals. None of that ghastly rock and roll stuff.'

Simon smiled inwardly. Anna was broad-minded and played all sorts of musical genres although her real love was for the classics. 'She likes the great composers, like Mozart.' Simon knew all about Moira the music tutor's view of Mozart's lifestyle. The great composer would never have been among Lady R-L's favourites.

'That is very good. Although I think I should draw your attention to something our dear vicar has told me.'

'Really?'

'The girl Anna is often seen around the village walking barefoot. That can only be a tendency to lax behaviour. We are not backward peasants.'

Lady Reece-Lamprey nodded and then stood up and left the office. Simon watched her walk away down the path to her house.

'Sorry about all that,' said Carl. 'She's all right really, but she does get some funny ideas.'

You can say that again, thought Simon. He wondered what her ladyship would say if she'd seen Lizzie chattering by the roadside topless or even Angie in her revealing sun dress. Lizzie had been caught reading a covert copy of Lady Chatterley; just as well her ladyship didn't know that. Simon didn't agree with Lady R-L, but his years of military service did make him allergic to sweaty feet even if, as it happened, all his three ladies were shoeless that hot day.

'Right,' said Carl. 'Can we talk about that new baler?'

Three months had passed and the heatwave was still with them although it was broken up by occasional refreshing thunderstorms. Angie was now fully pregnant and rounder in shape. Simon was pleased that she was following doctor's orders to the letter; cutting down on coffee as well as a whole range of food and of course no alcohol. The dread day could not be more than a month away. Angie seemed relaxed and casual but Simon could not share this. He pestered the doctor and others with questions about Angie's age and was reassured by everyone that his wife's age was much less of a factor these days.

The children were now far more interested in their mother's condition and both Simon and Angie had been amused by Lizzie's running a book on the gender of her future sibling. For ten new pence her friends could place a bet: boy or girl. Angie had been firm that any profit must go to a respectable charity.

One morning Angie collected the morning post. Simon had arranged for the letter slot in the door to have a basket attached to stop his wife bending to floor level. She had gathered up the letters and then retreated into the living room slamming the door behind her. Now Simon worried that her condition was making her irrational.

'All right, come in here. I've news for you,' she called.

Simon opened the door and went into the room. Anna held a letter in her hand and was giving him her best sardonic smile. That usually meant trouble.

'What?' he asked.

'This letter is from Cyprus. Your Melina has had a baby girl. She insists rather loudly that her Costas is the father.'

Simon knew better than to be angry or, uptight, as Lizzie would say. 'Surely that's good news.'

'All right,' now she laughed. 'It is just possible that you did the deed in England, but this time I think it is unlikely.'

'Much more than unlikely, believe me – impossible.'

Angie smiled. 'This time I really do believe you.'

Angie put down the letter and Simon walked across the room and kissed her.

CHAPTER 35

On the 27th July 1976 little Andrew Robsby was born in the maternity wing of the town hospital. For the first time Simon had been persuaded to be there in the birthing room. The ordeal had lasted several hours before he had staggered uncertainly down the hospital corridor to a pay phone. From here he had spread the news to his and Angie's families and to Bill his employer and to his and Angie's many friends in Shinkley and area. The other children were all home from school and in the care of the Kellingham family. They received the news but were more worried about their mother's health.

He returned to the room having spent more small change than a Yorkshire man would like. Angie lay with the new arrival, his tiny head on her exposed breast. 'Are you sure you're Ok?' he asked.

'No,' she whispered. 'I can't be until you stop looking like that and fussing. No, I feel fine – happier than I've ever been and you're a new dad again.'

'Well, he's a grand little fellah, but he's still a southerner,' Mary, Angie's mother gazed fondly at the new arrival now six weeks old. Little Andrew was a remarkably quiet infant and smiled a lot. 'Don't think he'll be a criminal,' said Simon. 'Not sure about being a soldier though.'

'Aye, but a true Yorkshire lad'd shout a bit more.'

Mary had finally steeled herself to make the trip to the alien South and had been driven by her son, Angie's younger brother, Arthur. He had taken a few days off from his well-paid job. Arthur had prospered as was indicated by his modern high-power Jaguar. Mary and husband Albert were not overjoyed by another aspect of Arthur's life. He was now engaged to a Lancashire girl; a betrayal not much less than his sister's settling in southern Sussex. Mary was well recovered from last year's mild stroke but she still limped a little especially after she first alighted from Arthur's swanky car.

At first Mary had looked around, eyes filled with dark suspicion until she found the village and the fields and hills not so very different to back home. 'Pretty little village you've got here,' she remarked. 'But the people; I suppose they're all "lah-di-dah – actually – I say – I

say – what's for luncheon?"' Mary's attempt to sound a bit like Jill Hilldown was not a success.

Angie hugged her. 'Mum, you'll find they're just the same as anywhere else. A lot of the people around here are farming folk. They're the ones Simon does his business with.'

Mary still looked doubtful.

Unlike the previous two births Simon had resolved to do his share of night work and nappy changing. Not a usual choice for a Yorkshire man but he didn't care. He hadn't reckoned with Lizzie who showed a remarkable skill with all tasks around a new born. Good experience for the future and recently she had declared an interest in qualifying for medical school. Lizzie fancied herself as a future surgeon. Both parents were determined that the older children should not feel left out and neglected. Mark clearly felt puzzled but Anna adored the new baby and the infant in turn was delighted when she gently sang to him.

Bill Gladstone had generously given Simon indefinite leave although Simon personally did not want to be away from the office for too long. Bill instead had gone out on the road himself and enjoyed meeting his customers on their farms. He admitted his sales figures had fallen in the absence of Simon.

Angie really was the strangest and the loveliest girl in the world. She insisted that he, Simon, must be the one to write and congratulate Melina on the birth of her little girl. If his wife had ever felt jealous or vindictive about his affair she never showed it. It seemed she viewed soldiers as soldiers, and soldiers overseas were rife for temptation. She made it more than clear that no future lapses would be tolerated. Nor would there be any lapses. Simon knew how lucky he was.

The family sent happy hours taking grandma' Mary around the area. She sat with Angie, plus Andrew in his special seat in the back of the Rover, while Simon drove with one or other of the older children in the passenger seat. Mary had treated these tours almost as if she was exploring a foreign land, which in her eyes she was. Gradually Mary's prejudices had eased. She saw the sights, met locals and had a good laugh with Barney the crusty regular in the Windy Ship pub. They pointed out the house once occupied by the Shartcroft and then the lodge and long driveway to the Blanner estate.

'That's nowt, we've posh houses like that in Yorkshire,' Mary was less than impressed.

Then all had suppressed excitement and driven past the BPP headquarters and Lizzie in the passenger seat had stuck her tongue out at the two burly skinhead guards. 'We should've taken old Bill with

us,' she said.

The older children were encouraged to get away from the home atmosphere of baby and smells and sail their little boats on the Harbour. This was a safe activity with the yacht club manning safety launches. They all loved the sailing; even Anna loved the boat although she worried about damaging fingers on the rope sheets. At this time of year the waters were warm, especially in the unusual hot weather, and the children revelled in capsize practice.

Mary stayed with them for ten days. She continued to mellow towards the South and all prejudice finally vanished when they took her to the annual village fete. Little Andrew came with the family and was admired by everyone. They watched the Morris dancers. The younger children laughed as they tried the skittles and coconut shy and archery, then finally the surprise of the day when Lizzie was awarded the title Miss Shinkley. Her parents had bought her a restrained dress that revealed nothing and had paid for her hair to be styled. The result was greeted with the warmest applause and pictures for the local paper. There was now no doubt. Their family was an established part of the life of Shinkley Common.

'You're right,' said Mary. 'I'd never have believed it, but folks down here is normal.'

'Well, of course they are,' said Simon. 'Mary, for heaven's sake we're all British, We all live in the same country.'

'Aye, seems in that you could be right.'

Two days later Arthur reappeared and Mary parted tearfully from the family and headed North again to her home turf.

'Grandma is so nice,' said Lizzie. 'She lives so far away. I shall miss her.'

'How about a trip north to Whitby,' said Simon. 'I know grandpa and grandma Robsby want to meet you as well.'

'I know,' said Lizzie. 'I've only seen them once and that was such a long time ago.'

'It was that day your father got his medal,' said Angie.

'Well, that wasn't all that long ago,' said Simon. Oh why was he suddenly thinking of Melina.

CHAPTER 36

'I'm very undecided,' said Angie. 'Stefanie from the commune was here earlier and she wants Anna to go to a children's party in that awful house.'

Simon was surprised. 'I'm not sure our girl will welcome that.'

Some of Anna's worst memories had been literally buried a year before. The police had released the burned body of, Nobby, Anna's murdered cat. Simon and Angie had arranged for the woodwork shop in the village to make a tiny sealed coffin. They had dug a grave in the furthest corner of their garden and then held a little ceremony. Anna had laid a rose on the box and the chapel minister had blessed her and the coffin. It had been some sort of closure and Anna had had fewer nightmares. Now these dark dreams had been almost left behind and her new parents were not inclined to do anything to revive them.

'From what I've heard,' said Angie. 'The new commune has completely redecorated inside the house and they've put in a new kitchen.'

'I doubt that would make it any easier for Anna,' replied Simon. 'But we can put the idea to her.'

'Yes,' said Angie. 'You see I had a most interesting talk a few weeks ago with Mrs Gentley. She's Tom Gentley's second wife. His first one died from a heart attack.'

'That's Sara Gentley isn't it?' said Simon. 'She's the one that writes books.'

'Did you know that Tom was a prisoner of war in the far-east and worked on the death railway?'

'No, I never knew that. He told me he'd been a sergeant in the war but that was all.'

'Sara said that when they first married Tom had regular night-mares. He was unable to sleep and was carried back in reality to that awful time. Then Sara was advised that the only cure was to go back and visit the places where he had witnessed these horrors.'

'Did that help?'

'Oh yes, Tom was actually keen to go in the end and they went. There they met comrades who had suffered with him and visited all the places where he had seen these crimes committed. Sara says they

134

came home and he's cured. He's never had another living-nightmare since.'

'So you think this might be a final closure for Anna?'

Angie frowned. 'I'm not claiming that. I'm not a bloody psychiatrist. But I think it might be the right thing to try.'

'All right, let's invite Steff and Tess over and they can talk to her.'

Simon and Angie with Andrew in her arms and all three children walked the short distance to the commune house. Lizzie and Mark were curious to see the inside of this once-sinister place, Anna understandably was nervous. Steffanie and Tessa had visited and spoken with her and she had been partly reassured because she knew them both and they were kind, so very different from Aunt Shartcroft. But the house itself held such bitter memory.

They reached the drive entrance and Angie took Anna's left hand and Lizzie held her right hand. Anna did not resist and they all walked slowly up to the house. To Simon it seemed a very ordinary place of similar 1930s architecture to their house and the Shartcroft banner above the front door had gone. Some trouble had been taken to tidy the garden and mow the front lawn. Simon was amused to think that this work must have been given to the girl's male partners. This was a wholly different world to the Shartcroft.

They reached the frontage, a wide gravel expanse filled now with parked cars. A group of children were jumping out of a yellow camper van. Anna suddenly smiled. 'They're my friends and Mike plays clarinet in our orchestra.'

She released her hands and ran across to her friends. Angie and Simon grinned; this was going to be all right. When Anna ran back to them she was smiling happily. 'Mike's my boyfriend from the orchestra.'

Boyfriend, thought Simon. Their little girl was barely fifteen. However this was no time for showing disapproval. The large front door was wide open and they could all hear the sounds of happy children's chatter.

'Aunt would never allow that door to be left open,' said Anna. 'She said men would stare at us from the road.'

I dare say they might, thought Simon. Just to get a glimpse of the mad cow.

Inside the house the hallway was bright with flowers and a crowd of happy children many of whom they all knew. Anna caught hold of Simon's hand. 'Upstairs, I'll show you where she made me sleep.'

In the end they were all taken by Anna on a tour of the house everywhere except the kitchen which held such dark memory. In fact apart from a small rear extension the place was identical to their home. They watched as Anna mixed happily with the other children, ate sticky cakes and joined in the games. Somehow both parents knew they were watching a miracle. Their darling adopted girl was exorcising her last demons. Her mistreatment would remain a memory for the rest of her life but the nightmares would be in the past. Not quite Tom Gentley's death railway but the same analogy.

The freak summer heatwave showed no signs of ending. It was refreshing to have an occasional noisy thunderstorm and a deluge of rain. The water was instantly absorbed by the dried farmland. The mood of the farmers, never cheerful, was especially gloomy although to Simon's eyes the corn crops looked good. The grassland was tinged with yellow but the grazing cattle and sheep still seemed to find it nourishing. In Late summer they heard the kids' exam results. Thank goodness Lizzie had passed her A levels with two distinctions and should qualify for university, and with a good chance that the university would be Oxford or Cambridge. Anna had done commendably in her test exams and she would be facing O Levels in the new-year. Mark had had a respectable result in the same tests but was clearly not as academic as his two sisters. But he had scored one hundred not out in a local village cricket match and everyone was proud of him for that. Here was one young member of the family with a military calling. Mark was now a corporal in the school Cadet Company and might eventually be following his father to Sandhurst.

Simon sat in his little office cubby hole. The windows were open and an electric fan struggled to stir some cool air in the enclosed space. Simon felt drowsy. Now the telephone was ringing.

He picked up the receiver and yawned but only for a second. The voice on the end of the line stiffened him with shock. 'Hello Simon, it is me, Melina.'

Oh no, where the hell was Angie? 'Melina, I think I told you not to contact me by telephone.'

'Of course, but do not worry I will do nothing to sadden your Angela. It is just that I go to work in Germany and Costas is coming with me with our own little Alexandra.'

Simon couldn't think of a reply. 'I hope you are happy and do well.'

'I do not think that we will ever meet again, but Simon I can tell

you, Costas is a good man and kind, but you,' there came a long pause. 'I loved you. I still love you and only you and I always will.'

Once again his senses alerted Simon fumbled for words. 'I was fond of you too and I will not forget you.'

They said goodbye and he heard a long audible kissing sound and then silence. Simon was on his feet and running upstairs. The phone extension was in place and there was no sign of the kid's tape recorder. Then he released a sigh of relief. There were no children because Angie was fetching them from school. With a bit of luck he would escape with his life.

'We haven't been to church for almost a month,' said Angie. 'How about showing our faces tomorrow?'

'Yes, all right,' said Simon. 'I haven't got anything better to do on Sunday anyway.'

The long heatwave had ended and now it was raining. The weather forecast spoke of a "complex area of low pressure". That apparently meant two or three days of low cloud and penetrating rain. So on Sunday they decided to drive to the chapel. Here they received a shock. Police cars and a police van were parked along the grass verge. A dozen uniformed coppers stood around looking menacing. What on earth? Simon wound down the car window and explained they were on their way to the chapel service.

'All right, you can pass.'

'What's all this about?' asked Simon.

'Seems, Mr Fircomb is saying a piece in your church about how he's discovered God.'

'And the BPP don't like him or God.'

'That's about it.' The copper waved them on.

'I'm not sure about this,' said Simon. 'Do you want to go home?'

'No,' said Angie. 'I say we go and listen to the man. We'll see if he's genuine.'

'What do you children think?'

Lizzie replied. 'I say we go in and hear the man.'

Simon settled for the majority vote and drove into the car park behind the chapel. It was already surprisingly full and among the potential congregation Simon recognised Sally Lederman from the local paper and her cameraman. The Robsby family walked to the front entrance. Simon looked back up the road to the middle of Shinkley. The police had closed the road in both directions with lines of dark-blue-clad officers. Now he could see a motley crowd of BPP

clad in dungarees and faces covered in masks. So, where was the repentant Fircomb? Simon remembered Fircomb from that village hall meeting about Europe. He was here but looked different, Mr Hobbs the minister was introducing everyone to an insignificant little man dressed in a sports jacket and grey flannels. He had a floppy brown hair style growing from what once Simon had assumed to have been either a shaved skinhead or a Hitler fringe. If the man had been in his old company he would have been ordered to have a haircut pronto. So this was the fearsome Fircomb who in a previous life would have cheerfully expelled half a million coloured immigrants and their families and reeked vengeance on the nation's Jews.

The man's statement of repentance rang true. Simon didn't know whether to be surprised or not. Fircomb had stated: "Like Paul on the Damascus road God came to me and opened my eyes. I learned that we are all children of God: Africans, Asians and Jews of whom Jesus was born one…" Fircomb went of to relate the story of the slave trader, John Newton who had also had a similar vision of God. All in all it was a moving confession and Simon had to admit it sounded genuine. The congregation stood and sang Newton's hymn: *Amazing Grace*. Neither Simon nor Angie wanted to accept the minister's invitation to meet and talk to Fircomb. All the children looked puzzled as their parents hurried them away to the car and home. 'Our group, we hated him,' said Lizzie. 'Now I'm not sure.'

Well, thought Simon. What would Shinkley throw up next?

138

CHAPTER 37

Anna had been invited to travel north with the National Youth Orchestra. She had been accepted for a full place in the strings section for the next year. She was nervous about leaving her secure home for a whole week, but then they discovered one of the concerts was to be held in the hall in Scarborough, just a stone's throw from Simon's family home near Whitby. This was their whole family's chance to travel north and meet Simon's people and then enjoy Anna's great moment and Anna would remain close to those she loved and made her feel secure.

'This place is fantastic,' said Lizzie. She was standing with her parents, Mark and little Andrew in his mother's arms. They were here on this fine early September day looking down over the town and harbour of Whitby. Behind them was the world-famous ruined abbey.

'This is where Dracula came disguised as a dog,' Simon grinned.

'You mean the blood-sucking bloke in that film.'

'No,' said Angie. 'Dracula was in a famous novel from a hundred years ago. But he's not around now.'

Simon laughed. 'I'd need my crack-shot corporal with a silver bullet.'

'Who's that statue bloke over there?' Lizzie pointed.

'That's Captain Cook. He discovered Australia.'

'What did he want to do that for?'

'Why not?'

''Cos it's full of Australians.'

'What's wrong with Australians?'

'Maisie in our school is an Aussie and she called me a slapper. Only because she wanted to go out with Nick and I got him first.'

Simon was filled with nostalgia as they looked down over this gem of a little town with its cobbled streets and the harbour with the broad expanse of the North Sea beyond. The neat little harbour, once a thriving fishing port, was now filled with expensive yachts. This was his home town. His mum and dad Henry and Rose had abandoned farming and were making a much better living with a nicely appointed small boarding house. Angie and he had stayed there in their courting

days and his parents had been firm in making them sleep in separate single rooms. His children had only met their grandparents once at his medal presentation. Lizzie had been young then and Mark too small to remember. Since then the family had been immersed in service life and then the complete change to settling in Shinkley and Sussex. It was so good to be back here with all his childhood memories. The only member of the family not with them was Anna. She was immersed in her orchestra's rehearsal in Scarborough. The family, apart from Andrew, would be going there later that evening to see Anna in the orchestra as it played Beethoven's Pastoral Symphony and another up-and-coming violinist played Mendelssohn's violin concerto. It was nice to think that it would be their Anna standing up there as soloist in a few years time.

The concert was well attended. The hall was much smaller than the theatre in Sussex but the acoustics were fine. Simon had been told that it was in this hall that Lady Reece-Lamprey had held a Northern rally. Tonight the whole family had come to see Anna, apart from little Andrew who was with his grandparents up the road in Whitby. Anna played in the second row of violins in an orchestra conducted on the night by a name that even Simon had heard of. Not normally a fan of the classics he knew that these were great works and he was wholly absorbed. Anna certainly looked confident as she watched the conductor's baton. The Mendelssohn concerto was fronted by a young boy soloist with long floppy hair. Simon strongly disapproved of the hair but was drawn into the performance and the lovely melodies. One day it would be their little girl standing playing this advanced work. Two hours later all the family walked together along the Scarborough waterfront. The moon was bright on the water and they could see the silhouette of the ruined castle cold and black on the hill. Lizzie pulled them all willingly into a fish and chip bar that was still open. Southerners now they might all be, but they knew that this Yorkshire fare was the finest in England.

They had two more days holiday in Whitby and then the children's school terms would recommence and they needed to be home. Home mused Simon – surely this was home, his childhood playground, the territory of his ancestors. Rough Vikings those ancestors may have been but they had left their stamp on this lovely corner of England. They sat on a bench, all five of them plus little Andrew in his father's arms. In front of them was the harbour of Whitby so familiar to

captain Cook and generations of fishermen. Today they could watch a religious service taking place to dedicate a newly-restored local trawler. A brass band was playing the hymn *For those in peril on the sea*. Simon had been a soldier but he knew this hymn and its lovely melody was symbolic of seafarers and their way of life.

Angie nudged him. 'Do you know the name of the melody of that hymn?'

'No, it's about the sea and the navy.'

'Well, the hymn is set to a melody and that melody is called – Melita.'

'Really,' he didn't know what to say and Angie had her mocking expression.

'Another thing,' she said. 'Melina is very like Melita and that is the real name for Malta, but your little girl is a Cypriot.'

'Yes, she told me in fact her mother was Maltese.'

Oh how Simon wished his wife would stop turning the knife in the wound. He knew he had been long forgiven and he wished the memory could be forgotten.

'I do like your mum and dad,' she continued. 'I always have, ever since our early days. We must invite them to come south to our home.'

'How about nearer Christmas – they can't leave the hotel now, it's still just about holiday season.'

'Good idea.' Angie leaned across and kissed his cheek.

Andrew was stirring and beginning to mew. 'I think he wants food,' said Simon.

Angie grinned. 'I think I'll slip across to that bus shelter.'

'Why?'

Lizzie giggled. 'So the whole world won't see him sucking her titties.'

He glared at his daughter. 'That will do.'

Angie stood up and took Andrew in her arms. 'Lizzie, just you wait. You and Anna; it'll only be a few years, God willing, and you'll be feeding your own kids.

Both Lizzie and Anna laughed. 'Yes,' said Lizzie. 'And then you'll be granny.'

Two days later Simon turned off the main road and into the Shinkley street. It had clearly been raining but the village was now bathed in a warm autumnal sun. Another hundred yards and they all saw their house. Simon parked in front of the garage. 'That's it we're home.'

'It's been three years in the South,' said Angie 'And so much has happened. But you're right this is our home; home for us all and there'll never be anywhere else.'

'I've been so lucky,' said Simon. 'I loved my army career but these three years have been the best in my life.'

'You don't want to go back up north?'

'Not any more. This is Sussex and this is our home.'

THE END

By the same author

THE NEMESIS FILE

Professional yachtsman and Olympic medallist Steve Simpson has problems. His wife has died and his Chichester sail making business is under threat. When Steve and his daughter Sarah find the body of a young Dane in the sea off the Sussex coast they are inextricably sucked into an international blackmail and drugs conspiracy.

The story describes fourteen days in the late summer of 1990 that will change Steve's life. It is a test that leads him to new love and a rebirth of his hopes.

This tense mystery-thriller moves swiftly from Sussex to Copenhagen with interludes in Portsmouth, Italy and Scotland, and ends with a sea chase in a gale

ISBN 978-0-9548880-0-8 (0-9548880-0-6)

Available from Benhams Books
1 Fir Cottage, Greatham, Liss, Hampshire GU33 6BB

Reviews of *The Nemesis File*:

Journalist Pamela Payne: With locations as diverse as the South Coast of England, Naples and Denmark, *The Nemesis File*'s credible sailing scenes will either have you reaching for the seasickness-pills or signing on for a course; the sex scenes, however, are the most romantic I have read for along time. A great adventure story, which will delight both sexes – sailors or landlubbers."

Yachts and Yachting December 2004. "...Jim Morley is a sailor writing for sailors and his first novel is immersed in the South Coast yachting and dinghy scene...if somebody was going to write a novel for *Yachts and Yachting,* readers this would probably be it.

Yachting Monthly: 2006. Dell Quay based yachtsman Jim Morley has turned his hand to writing thrillers based on his sailing experiences of forty years. His first novel, *The Nemesis File,* is a murder mystery linking a Chichester sailmaker with a failing business, the corpse of a Dane found floating off Sussex and Nazi propaganda minister Josef Goebbels.

Reviews of *The Nemesis File* (continued):

Olympic sailor and coach: Cathy Foster, 11th Dec 2004

Rarely have I read such a racy book! It's carries you along at pace, and holds you fast until the very end. Just then, you think that maybe this is getting far-fetched, but the punch-line pulls you up short, and makes you re-assess the characters and their relationship to events. Suddenly the plot hangs together again in a very satisfactory way, just as good detective stories should.

Instead of long descriptions to 'paint a picture' of all the venues and situations, the writing is succinct and carefully crafted to give the maximum impression for the minimum words. This gives the book its fast tempo, yet nothing is lost because the accurate detailing of locations and action bonds the reader into plot. As a past Olympic sailor myself, I know the sailing venues described in both Chichester Harbour and Copenhagen well, and I can reassure any future reader that the author has definitely done his research. In addition, he's right – you do build life-long bonds with other British athletes and other countries' sailors when you are part of the Olympic team representing your country. It is a pleasure and highly unusual to read a book which describes the joys of sailing and racing so well. Yet it's not a book about sailing, full of technicalities of the sport. Sailing provides the background framework for a story of murder and blackmail where the investigation chases over four countries and three generations of lives. A thoroughly enjoyable read.

Cathy Foster went to the Olympics in 1984 (finished 7th and made history as the first woman helm since the 2nd World War) and competed in two other Olympic campaigns, the last being 2002/3. She's a freelance Coach who specialises in top level racing, including Olympic and Paralympic sailors

By the same author

ROCASTLE'S VENGEANCE

When out of work sea captain Peter Wilson takes a job as harbour master in the Dorset yacht harbour of Old Duddlestone, he is surprised to learn that his own father, James Wilson, was the harbour's wartime commander.

There are unsolved crimes involving this secretive community dating back fifty years. The deaths of the entire personnel of a research laboratory, then a rape and murder followed by a lynching.

Peter, aged ten, witnessed his father's suicide. Now he hears disquieting rumours about his father's dubious activities in Duddlestone. He forms a relationship with single-mother, Carol Stoneman. When Carol's ten-year-old son is abducted, Peter is forced into a situation that nearly bring his own destruction.

This mystery thriller is set on the Dorset coast in the summer of 1997, with a sailing background.

ISBN 978-0-9548880-1-5 (0-9548880-1-4)

Available from Benhams Books
1 Fir Cottage, Greatham, Liss, Hampshire GU33 6BB

Reviews of *Rocastle's Vengeance*:

Unsolicited comment on Amazon. *****
Wow! What a read. You know it is a good book when after a few pages you don't want to put it down, nor answer the phone, door or anything...

Bournemouth Echo, July 2006.
Novelist brings mystery to the coast.
Rocastle's Vengeance, James Morley's second novel, is brimming with references to Purbeck Poole and Bournemouth. The book recounts the tale of a harbour master who uncovers murky secrets when he takes a job in the imaginary village of Old Duddlestone...

Tim O'Kelly. Whitbread Prize judge southern region.
Jim Morley writes with skill and intelligence: a genuine storyteller in the finest tradition.

MAGDALENA'S REDEMPTION

If an eight-year-old boy commits murder is he irredeemably evil? Can he ever be rehabilitated or will he kill again to preserve his secret?

Hampshire farmer, Tom O'Malley, finds the dead body of a young journalist. Not satisfied that she is a suicide he makes his own investigation.

Fed rumours about his friend and employer, Hollywood film director Gustav Fjortoft, he angrily rejects them. Yet all his inquiries into his friend's past seem to substantiate the rumours.

Following suspicious deaths in his own community, Tom's quest leads him the American West Coast, where he escapes abduction and near death.

Returning to England he finds the answers he seeks in a dramatic finale in his home village.

ISBN 978-0-9548880-2-2

EMILY'S HOUR

Everything changes for the Simpson family when the dead body of an internet millionaire is found in Branham Lake and a close friend is falsely accused of murder.

It is 2004 and Steve and Kirsten, the central characters in James Morley's first novel, The Nemesis File are now married and have settled in rural Sussex with their children Emily 13 and John-Kaj 8. Steve runs the family nautical business near Chichester but teaches sailing at Branham Lake on the Surrey Hampshire border.

When further deaths occur, a police inspector facing a mental breakdown is convinced of his suspect's guilt. While Steve and Kirsten fight to clear their friend's name they have no inkling of the nightmare that is to engulf them. When Emily, along with an elderly war veteran, is abducted by a sacrificial religious cult, the family become the centre of worldwide attention.

Emily's Hour is a tense thriller, with a background in sailing that will engage both adults and teenagers alike

ISBN 978-0-9548880-3-9

Available from Benhams Books
1 Fir Cottage, Greatham, Liss, Hampshire GU33 6BB

By the same author

OLYMPIC NEMESIS

Emily Simpson's Olympic dream is threatened by an internet gambling syndicate.

Emily and crewmates Chloë and Erin are selected to sail for Britain in games held in the mysterious South American country of Olifa. Emily's father, Steve, is sailing in the Paralympics. Speculation about a father/daughter double gold puts both under threat.

Former Olympian Steve recovers from a stroke to rediscover his love of sailing.

Emily's Danish mother, Kirsten, lives in the shadow of her family's wartime disgrace. Rumours circulating about Emily's ancestry bring her and partner, Tom, into danger from a deluded stalker.

ISBN 978-0-9548880-4-6

FLANAGAN'S LEGACY

An international conspiracy in 1919. The killing of children in a Spanish village in 1937. Distant events come back to haunt the lives of Clare O'Dwyer and Michael Walters a young couple unborn at the time of either.

It is the early summer of 1994. Clare has inherited the fortune of her grandfather: US Senator James O'Dwyer, war hero, rogue politician and last survivor of the Flanagan Plot. Even after seventy years the truth would cause a fatal breach in relations between the United States and Britain.

Clare has no knowledge of this plot but is not believed. She is threatened by both security services and terrorists. To escape the pair run away to sea in their sailing yacht *Quadra*. The voyage takes them from France, Dorset, Cornwall and finally West Cork. They are abducted by terrorists and survive a force ten gale off Southern Ireland. In a dramatic climax Michael narrowly escapes with his life and Clare discovers something about her grandfather that will change her life for ever.

ISBN 978-0-9548880-5-3

Available from Benhams Books
1 Fir Cottage, Greatham, Liss, Hampshire GU33 6BB

By the same author

TANGLED RETRIBUTION

Did a half-million dollar bribe to throw a yacht race lead to the brutal murder of a yachtmaster?

Why should this threaten Emily Stoneman and her newborn baby?

When further murders occur it seems a psychopath is loose. Yacht journalist David Manning makes his own investigations with startling results.

Tangled Retribution is a tense detective novel involving characters from James Morley's previous sailing thrillers.

ISBN 978-0-9548880-6-0

SONG OF SUSSEX

Song of Sussex is a new departure for James Morley. A historical saga covering most of the last century and some of this.

The story is the fictional life of Richard Dyer, a boy born on a Sussex farm in 1920. Richard has a gift for music that takes him from humble birth to world-wide fame. The story has something for everyone: music, 1930s London, flying with the RAF in World War 2, then the post-war world where Richard achieves his triumph.

Richard has a tangled love life that causes his Australian wife, Stella to drag him back to her homeland. The story ends with Richard the farm boy honoured in every country and continent. The city of Chichester and the county of Sussex resonate through the story. And there is plenty of sailing.

ISBN 978-0-9548880-7-7

Available from Benhams Books
1 Fir Cottage, Greatham, Liss, Hampshire GU33 6BB